"I like

Grant placed squeeze. "I like how you stay so positive when it looks as if we're at a dead end."

"We are no such thing," Marie assured him. "Something will pop, you'll see."

She leaned over and kissed him. The act surprised her almost as much as it did him.

She felt his lips tense, then relax and welcome hers. Passion flared.

She closed her eyes. He'd find out soon enough she wasn't all she was advertising, but she did want this kiss and she wanted it badly.

Whatever happened next would just have to happen.

Dear Reader,

Who doesn't love to travel! Holland is one of my favorite places to vacation. The best I could do this year was to go there vicariously through my hero and heroine and demand a lengthy trip report. It's a wonderful country full of lovely sights and friendly people. I highly recommend it.

Where do the book ideas come from? All over the place this time. I chose the locations. Research into terrorism in the Netherlands and an abnormal psych book gave me the villains. My granddaughter, who was eager to get me away from the computer to play, suggested "a kidnapping with a really mean bad guy and lots of love stuff since it *is* a romance." (Thanks, hon, you might have a future in this business.)

I love writing about strong women who can take care of themselves. I love overprotective heroes, bless their great big macho hearts. And I really love it when the two claim each other against their better judgment and the rules of the game.

Go romance!

Lyn Stone

LYN STONE

Claimed by the Secret Agent

Silhouette®
Romantic
SUSPENSE

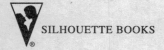 SILHOUETTE BOOKS

Recycling programs
for this product may
not exist in your area.

ISBN-13: 978-0-373-27622-6
ISBN-10:   0-373-27622-2

CLAIMED BY THE SECRET AGENT

Books by Lyn Stone

Silhouette Romantic Suspense
Beauty and the Badge #952
Live-In Lover #1055
A Royal Murder #1172
In Harm's Way #1193
Down to the Wire #1281
Against the Wall #1295
Under the Gun #1330
Straight Through the Heart #1408
From Mission to Marriage #1444
Special Agent's Seduction #1449
Kiss or Kill #1488
The Doctor's Mission #1534
Claimed by the Secret Agent #1552

*Special Ops

LYN STONE

is a former artist who developed an early and avid interest in criminology while helping her husband study for his degree. His subsequent career in counterintelligence and contacts in the field provided a built-in source for research in writing suspense. Their long and happy marriage provided firsthand knowledge of happily-ever-afters.

This book is dedicated to Rebecca Renae Clair.

Thank you so much for your time and
very helpful suggestions.

Prologue

McLean, Virginia—July 11

"The Embassy Kidnapper struck another consulate yesterday, but he grabbed the wrong Yank this time," Jack Mercier declared. "Marie Beauclair is CIA, working out of the consulate in Munich as a translator." He sat back in his chair and crossed his arms. "The Company won't be sending anyone after her."

"Why not? She wouldn't be marked as one of theirs just because they rescued her," Grant Tyndal asked.

Mercier was going to send him after the woman. Made sense. Though he worked for COMPASS now, his six years with a navy SEAL team had given him the most experience in hostage extractions. This mission would almost feel like a personal quest, with its similarities to one that had happened when he was a kid. Kidnapping, Germany, young blond victim, family and authorities passing off the responsibility for getting her back. Then, he had been powerless to do anything.

"CIA turned it over to us," Mercier said, interrupting his thoughts. "We have a better chance of stopping these abductions than the Company does, especially if we get Beauclair back alive. Mainly we're doing it because I *want* her," Mercier stated.

Grant pursed his lips and stifled any further questions. Mercier had a wife, a gorgeous woman with a medical degree and a mesmerizing French accent. What? Was he crazy?

"Not personally," the boss said with a roll of his eyes. "I had requested her transfer to us. Beauclair has a photographic memory and is a wizard with languages. The consul General sent us her file and suggested she was being underused where she was. She'll be a valuable asset to COMPASS."

True. All his fellow agents had their special little gifts. His particular gig was psychometry. He might get a sense of what the young woman had been feeling or thinking if he could hold something she had owned, but that sense wouldn't help him find her if she hadn't known where she was going when she'd been taken. "Does she have a locator implant?"

Mercier nodded and nudged a folder across the desk. "Here are her coordinates. The jet's waiting, and there will be a car available as soon as you land. Get her out and keep it as quiet as possible."

"And after the extraction?" Grant asked as he lifted the folder and glanced at the photo of the agent. Who smiled that way for an I.D. badge photo? And who ever looked that good in one? He knew how deceiving appearances could be. If she'd made it through CIA training, she was no lightweight, either in smarts or capability. She was twenty-eight and looked eighteen. On purpose, he'd bet.

"First, get her to safety. Then I want you to go after this guy before he snatches somebody else. We should have been called in on this sooner. Beauclair is victim number five. We think he's using the ransoms to help fund his jihad. Or maybe this *is* his jihad. Find out if he's working alone or in concert with some group."

All the U.S. embassies and consulates were made aware of the kidnappings three weeks ago, since the perp had been skipping all over the globe. If his victim was ransomed, he'd dump her, tied up naked and helpless, in a public park where she would soon be found alive after the money was delivered. The last vic had been tortured and killed when the ransom was denied. "So this one can't be ransomed."

"Not officially. You know U.S. policy about dealing with terrorists. And her family doesn't have the money or any assets to convert."

The only dead victim had made a point—*don't pay, don't get them back alive.*

Mercier stood and offered his hand. "Report every twenty-four hours or we'll come looking for you."

"I know the drill," Grant replied. He had completed two assignments for COMPASS during the year he'd been with the team and hadn't needed any help. After six years in the navy, running missions of all descriptions and feeling responsible for every one of his team every hour of the day, Grant reveled in working alone.

This antiterrorist organization was a tightly knit group, but each member was trusted to handle an assignment the way he or she saw fit. Backup was available for the asking, and rescue, if required, was speedy. They didn't partner up unless the mission called for it.

Mercier motioned him out. He didn't say goodbye or good luck. That was one of his peculiarities. He must figure encouragement wasn't needed. Or maybe he feared he would jinx things.

Grant dismissed the thought and began to think ahead about Agent Marie Beauclair of the wide blue eyes and dimples and how best to rescue her.

He welcomed the chance, as he always did, but this one felt almost personal. Finding her couldn't make up for his inability to save Betty Schonrock when he was thirteen. Nothing could do that. He'd always carry the guilt. But he'd do this in memory of Betty and maybe it would help a little.

Chapter 1

Germany—July 15

Marie Beauclair focused on the narrow field of vision beneath the blindfold. Not a big room, low ceiling, high, narrow window. The air was cave cold, not the result of air-conditioning. It chilled her all over.

The first thing she'd realized when she'd come to was that she was nearly naked. Her wrists and ankles were tied with cord, and she lay on a cot that smelled musty. Her next stage of awareness was absolute fury. She was mad as hell at the jerk who had done this and almost as mad at herself for letting him. How had it happened?

She couldn't remember a thing after coming home from work on Monday, changing out of her work clothes, pulling on a tank top and going to the fridge for a glass of orange juice. Nothing else, not even falling as she passed out. Drugged, of course, with something really fast acting. Then she dimly recalled someone lifting her head, urging her to drink more. How long had she been here, and how many times had she drank the stuff?

Her head wasn't clear even now, but she was conscious and thinking. Deep breathing helped shake off the lethargy. She flexed her muscles and stretched her neck as best she could to work out the kinks. Her stomach rumbled, and her mouth felt as dry as dust.

Marie listened to the rising voice in the next room, a one-sided conversation in accented Dutch, obviously a phone call. She recorded the content, storing each word as she tried to work her wrists out of the cord that bound her.

Essentially he was discussing where he should dump her if the ransom wasn't paid. And it wouldn't be; Marie knew that much. This had to be the Embassy Kidnapper, and his demand was exorbitant.

She couldn't lie here and wait for a rescue that might not happen.

When the voice stopped, so did she, knowing it was imperative that she remain motionless except for slow, even breathing and feign unconsciousness. If he knew she was awake, he'd have to deal with her. She was pretty sure who had grabbed her and what the end result would be.

The door creaked open and she sensed him approach. He poked her sharply in the ribs. She didn't react. He checked her bonds, grunted with satisfaction, then paused as he turned to leave, as if he were thinking about what to do next.

Through the crack in the blindfold, Marie caught a good view of his profile—dark complexion, black hair and full lips. She glimpsed a raised scar on the back of his wrist when he raked a hand through his hair. He looked Middle Eastern, but the accent she had heard didn't bear that out.

He paced for a moment, then cursed under his breath and left the room. She heard the door click shut and a dead bolt turn, then his footsteps. Another door slammed shut. She listened for further sounds from the next room and heard nothing.

Here was her chance, and it might be the only one she got. Furiously, she worked the cords, curling her thumbs into her palms until one hand slipped free, and then she tore at the cords that bound her ankles.

He had locked the door. No point in bothering with that. She headed straight for the window. It wasn't barred, only painted black. And painted shut, Marie discovered when she stood on a chair to open it. Quickly, she jumped down, picked up the chair and used it to break the panes.

Great. She couldn't go through that jagged opening with so much skin exposed. After a quick glance around the room, she grabbed the only fabric she could find, the moth-eaten blanket that had covered the cot.

She padded her hand with the threadbare wool and broke out all the glass she could, then draped the ragged thing over the bottom of the window frame. It took her nearly five minutes, by her reckoning, to squeeze her body through the opening and jump down into the dark alley. Shards cut her feet when she landed, but there was no help for that.

She snatched up the old blanket and wrapped it around her. Then she ran like hell, still weaving from the aftereffects of the drug in her system.

She had no clue where she was, but anywhere was better than back *there*.

Her feet were bleeding and leaving a trail, but she ran on, ignoring the pain of the cuts. Desperation fueled her, but she didn't let herself panic. She needed a clear head, time to think, to find out where she was and to plan.

It was either dusk or predawn; she couldn't tell. Nearly dark, whatever the time. Warehouses. Old ones. Probably no dwellings nearby. Cobblestones. Old town. Had to have a center. She needed people. Crowds.

The end of the long alley lay just ahead. She sucked in a deep breath and slowed her pace. Suddenly a hand clapped over her mouth and a strong arm clamped her waist, yanking her backward into a hard body.

She went limp, hands behind her, and when the hold on her relaxed, she struck. Her fingers dug into his most vulnerable part, twisting as hard as she could.

He let go and she took off, seeking the faint light of the street, praying there would be help there.

But he snatched her again, this time by her upper arms, and dragged her back. "Dammit! Don't fight me! I'm here to *help!*"

It took a few seconds for his words to register. His lack of accent. His *Americaness*. "Thank God," she muttered, and collapsed.

"Wake up, Beauclair!" She heard the command before her eyes opened and groaned her assent. He had her sitting on his lap against the wall of the alley and was tapping her face with his hand.

She reached up, batted it away and struggled to get up. "Who sent you?"

He stood, lifting her with him as he did. "Later. Right now, we should get out of here before he realizes you're gone."

"Aren't you armed?" she demanded, reaching for the blanket that had slipped away. Modesty was not her primary concern at the moment, but she was cold.

"Yeah, but I need to get you safely situated before I go after him." He put his palm on her waist.

She knocked his hand away. "Like hell. I want a piece of that—"

"Whoa, tiger!" She heard his chuckle. "Serve him right if I did turn you loose on him. You nearly killed *me*."

"Sorry. Sneak up on a girl, expect that."

"Makes me wonder how he grabbed you in the first place."

"Drugged me," she explained defensively as she tucked the blanket snugly around her like a sarong. "He's the Embassy Kidnapper, right?"

"The M.O. sure fits. The car's half a block down. Can you walk?" He held out a hand to assist, but she avoided it.

"I can run if I have to. I just did."

"Good for you. Let me check the street first. Watch the alley behind us."

Dawn had broken now. The street was deserted except for the two of them hurriedly making their way to his vehicle.

As soon as she was inside, Marie leaned her head back on the headrest and released a heavy sigh of relief.

When she opened her eyes, he was staring at her. "You okay?" he asked, real concern in his voice. "He didn't—"

Marie interrupted the question and met his worried gaze dead on. "I heard him talking in the next room when I woke up. He's not working this alone."

"I didn't see him leave, but there's a door at the front of the building, too."

He started the car, and soon they were bumping down a narrow street. The ancient structures that abutted it were shuttered and looked abandoned. She fiddled with the seat belt and finally got it fastened. "Where are we and what time is it?"

"A little village, Bad Nutzbach or something. It's barely 5:00 a.m. and it's Sunday, in case you don't know."

"Thanks. Now who the hell are you, and where are we going?"

He made a right turn and sped up. "Grant Tyndal. I'm with COMPASS. You familiar with it?"

She nodded but didn't elaborate. So the Company hadn't seen fit to come after her. She hadn't expected her family to do anything to help her, even if they had been rolling in money, but she had thought the CIA might. Instead this guy shows up from the antiterrorist team that had recently offered her a position. "Am I supposed to feel obligated now to accept the job offer?"

He glanced at her and smiled. "Of course. This is how

we *always* recruit. As to your other question, we're going to the hospital in Landstuhl and get you checked out. You'll be flying stateside before you know it."

"I'm not leaving until I catch him."

Tyndal's laugh annoyed her. "Don't think so. I work alone." His words annoyed her even more.

"Go to work, then. Just don't get in my way."

"Not exactly dressed for action, are you?" He had them flying down the autobahn by this time, doing at least ninety.

Marie pulled the blanket closer around her neck. She reluctantly admitted to herself that she needed his help. He wouldn't take her to her apartment. That was probably a designated crime scene by now.

She didn't have her creds or her weapon or any pockets to put them in. He could get all that for her if she played her cards right. And he surely had more information on the abductions than she could get on her own. She'd have to make it worth his while to partner up on this.

"Tell you what," she said, abandoning her defensive attitude for a conciliatory tone. "I can pull my weight. Let me in on this, and maybe I'll come on board with COMPASS when we're done. I have information you can use. Get me something to wear, a gun and I.D., and let's go after him together. Now."

She wasn't above using coercion. She put a tentative hand on his arm and squeezed. "Please?"

He glanced at her hand and then at her smile. But he didn't look as if he'd give an inch. "You're going to the hospital, Beauclair. You need an exam, a drug test and a rape kit."

Yes, well, there was that. She had bruises in all the right places, and that made her even madder. That bastard *had* raped the victim he'd killed. Not the others, though. If the reports could be believed.

She didn't think she'd been raped, but the fact that she'd been drugged, manhandled and made helpless was reason enough to want her kidnapper's head on a plate. Right along with whoever was giving him orders. She quickly dismissed that line of thinking so she wouldn't give herself away to Tyndal.

"After the exam?" she asked.

"I'll officially debrief you and call in the results. Then you go home. To the States. You're from Atlanta?"

She ignored the query. Since he'd been sent after her, he'd know that. "Look, I'm okay and perfectly capable of helping you catch this guy. I've actually *seen* him, and I know his voice. Will you at least consider it? Maybe request my help officially?" she asked, trying to suppress her anger and sound sweet. "Because if you don't, I might not have anything else to say to you."

"Obstruction of justice. Familiar with that phrase? It can send you to jail," he warned. Then her earlier statement seemed to register. "You can identify him?"

"Yes."

"Then we'll get an artist to work with you, but that's as far as you can go on this."

Marie retreated, but she didn't surrender. She never surrendered. There was always a way. She'd simply take another tack. "How far are we from Landstuhl?"

"About thirty miles."

She could see pretty well now even though it was

going to be a gray day and would probably rain soon. "Take me to the nearest *krankenhaus* instead. My feet are bleeding and I'm dehydrated."

Stealing a vehicle might be necessary to get away from him, and that would be easier in a small hospital not peopled with soldiers.

He immediately moved to the far right lane and took the next exit. For a few minutes she thought she was getting her way, but he pulled off on a side road and stopped the car.

She watched him reach into the backseat and retrieve a gray plastic box. "First-aid kit. Brought it in case we needed it when I found you."

He pushed his seat back all the way and then unhooked his seat belt and hers. "Turn sideways and put your feet in my lap."

"No!"

"I'm a qualified medic. Worst foot, please."

Marie's muscles were almost too tense to move, but she managed to turn. He helped her lift her legs and took her left foot in both his hands. She barely managed not to jerk it out of his grasp.

His glance raked her thighs before she could cover them with the blanket. Was it prurient, or was he checking for damage? Hard to tell. He didn't look all that salacious, but the old paranoia had kicked in.

"There's no telling what you stepped on in that alley," said, his tone gentle, almost a drawl.

She noticed his accent for the first time. It was faint but still there. Probably hadn't registered before because it was so close to her own. "You're from the South. Where?"

"Alabama. Anniston, originally. Army brat, though, so I lived all over the place." His hands were gentle as he continued examining her feet. "We'd better get these cuts cleaned up a little and wrapped before we go any farther. Uh-huh, that one might need a few stitches. Don't want a nasty infection."

He opened his door and slid out from under her feet. A moment later he returned with two bottles of water, one of which he handed her to drink. Setting the other on the ground, he then ripped the plastic off a roll of paper towels.

"Hand me the kit and get as comfortable as you can. I expect this will hurt a little bit," he warned.

Marie remembered she should sip the water slowly. She shuddered in spite of herself when he uncapped the other bottle of water to pour over her feet.

She sipped again, feeling the coolness slide all the way down to her empty stomach. "Consider it payback…since I hurt you." She slid down farther in the seat so that her feet were sticking outside the car on his side. "Go ahead."

His touch was light considering the size of his hands, but she didn't like to be touched, not by him or anyone else.

He was large all over, she noted, not just his hands. She'd have to stay aware. "Ow…ow…ow!" she yelped.

"There. I doused them with peroxide, too. That ought to do until you get them debrided. Like I said, you might need stitches in the left one." He proceeded to wrap both her feet in gauze. "Go ahead, sit up and finish the water. I'll find you something to put on."

He disappeared and she heard him open the trunk

again. In a few minutes he returned and tossed her a pair of socks and black sweats. "These will swallow you whole, but at least you'll be rid of that scratchy blanket. Don't take anything off but that. Roll it up and I'll bag it."

He shrugged and stuck his hands in the back pockets of his jeans. "I'll just...wait back there while you dress. Unless you need help?"

"I'll manage," she gasped. Marie grabbed the clothes and wrestled them on as quickly as she could.

He was surprisingly thoughtful. Maybe he was softening to the idea of letting her work with him. Or not. He probably thought she was a big baby. She swiped the tears from her face when she realized she'd been crying. Dammit. She never cried.

"All done?" he asked before looking inside.

"Ready," she said, hating the thickness of tears in her voice.

He got back in and handed her an energy bar to eat. Then he put the old blanket in a paper bag he'd brought. "Evidence," he explained as if she didn't know. Then he promptly started the car and drove back onto the autobahn. "Feeling better?"

"I told you I'm *fine*. Thanks for the clothes." She fell quiet then, bit into the energy bar and just watched him, really assessing him closely for the first time.

He radiated confidence and was probably very good at his job, judging by his actions thus far. He had taken that painful squeeze and twist she'd given his *essentials* with the good grace not many men would.

He was unusual in other ways, too. Not lecherous or superior for one thing. Most men saw her as fair game and, at the very least, offered suggestive looks or a condescending attitude. Usually both.

Marie knew how she looked and used it, even enhanced it to the max. That helped in her job as an undercover operative. It was actually difficult to present a different impression than little blond airhead because she stayed in that character so much of the time.

She was short and slightly built. Dainty, some called her. Dimples, baby-doll features and pale blond hair had always caused her more trouble than not, but they also gave her that necessary edge. She had mastered the wide-eyed, vacant-headed smile, complete with a self-deprecating little laugh of incomprehension. She must look pretty rough right now, but that should have piqued his sympathy if nothing else. So far, he'd treated her like a fellow agent who had just been through a rough time. Unusual and, she admitted, very welcome.

People, especially men, never gave her credit for a brain; yet not once had Tyndal talked down to her. So maybe he didn't make automatic assumptions based on appearance.

Neither did she, but she couldn't help noticing how he looked. Impossible not to. Maybe she'd seen better-looking guys in her time, but he certainly was no slouch in that department. In fact, he had a commanding presence, sort of rugged and suave at the same time. His voice was a bit gravelly and had that slight Southern drawl. In your face, but with a smile, that was him.

His hair was salt and pepper, obviously graying early, since the rest of him looked early to midthirties. The eyes were light, either gray or blue, and really intense.

Good strong nose and his mouth… Well, that mouth… didn't matter, she told herself firmly and jerked her gaze away from his profile.

Her overall impression was that Agent Tyndal was hot as hell, self-assured with good reason. And as stubborn as mule, she'd bet. A real challenge.

Now then, what would be the best way to appeal to him? How could she persuade him to let her go after these kidnappers without giving him the impression that her reason was personal? It *was* personal. Nobody yanked her around like a helpless rag doll anymore and got away with it. Nobody! If she let that happen again, it negated all her years of hard work, all that she had become.

She had to devise something before he put her on a plane back to the States. No way would she let that happen. She'd disappear first, and she damn well knew how.

Chapter 2

He wasn't going to budge. Marie decided that if she disappeared in Landstuhl, she'd be found almost immediately, so she had to go to plan B. She had to play it weak if her plan was to work. She brushed a hand over her face, sighed and shook her head. "Could I ask you a huge favor?"

"What?" He sounded a tad suspicious.

She upped the weak factor a notch. "I really need to go by my apartment when we get to Munich, just for a few minutes. Could we please do that?"

"All your stuff will probably have been packed up by now. I'm sure someone is detailed to bring your clothes and toiletries to the airport. I can call and check."

Again, she sighed before answering. "No, that won't

do. You see, it's my grandmother's ring. I really need to get it, and I know it's still there. It's pretty valuable. I keep it hidden away when I'm not wearing it, and whoever cleared my place won't have found it. Please? I *need* to have that."

Marie could feel Tyndal's gaze on her, assessing the truth of her motive. She looked up at him, eyes wide and pleading, the best little-girl-lost look she could do.

He shrugged. "Well, if we just run in and get it, I guess it would be okay."

"Thanks so much. It means so much to me." She hesitated, then added, "Maybe I could just take a quick shower while we're there?" She offered him a wry little smile and ran a hand through her hair. "I hate to stay this way."

He looked sympathetic. "Sure. That should be all right."

Piece of cake. Acting ability intact! Satisfied, she snapped on her seat belt, leaned against the window and settled in to take a nap on the way to the hospital.

Grant took a good, long look at her for the first time as she exited the exam room. It seemed before he'd only taken in bits and pieces of her at the time—dirty face, big round china-blue eyes, messy hair, cut-up feet and a milk-white length of exposed leg.

Now she stood there, eyeing him with a mixture of mistrust and gratitude that defied description. He didn't think he'd ever seen a woman combine those two expressions while looking at him.

She looked like a little warrior queen, battered but undefeated, absolutely driven to thrive and to seek retribution. That determination would fade, he knew. As soon as the adrenalin rush subsided, and it would, she'd probably collapse in tears and be perfectly willing to get as far away from Germany as was humanly possible.

But right now she was a picture to behold, so tiny in his oversize sweats and socks, one hand on her hip while the other impatiently raked the tousled blond curls back off her brow.

For a minute he saw Betty Schonrock, the first girl he'd ever loved. Beauclair had that same challenging lift of the chin. Aside from both having blond hair and small frames, the resemblance ended there. She wasn't Betty, but seeing Beauclair safe and knowing he'd had a hand in it caused a little of the weight to lift off his chest.

He had been head over heels for Betty, who'd been almost four years older, a senior at Frankfurt American High School when he was a lowly freshman. She had only spoken to him a few times, smiled at him now and then and rarely gave him a second look, but he'd loved her anyway.

Suddenly she had disappeared without a trace. Everyone thought she was a runaway and the investigation hadn't lasted even a week. Grant had never believed that Betty, a popular cheerleader and straight-A student about to graduate, would simply take off without a word and leave her charmed life behind. He was convinced she'd been abducted, but no one would listen to a thirteen year old who hadn't even known her that well.

His limited psychometric ability had failed him then, and so had his nearly nonexistent power of persuasion. But he had found *this* girl in time, and she was safe now.

Wherever you are, Betty, this one's for you. He felt marginally better.

"How did it go?" he asked Beauclair. Probably not the most tactful question considering she'd just undergone an examination for possible rape, but he needed to know.

"No damage. I'm okay," she said, defenses up like a nearly visible force field.

He doubted she was anywhere near okay but nodded his approval anyway. "Great, I'm glad to hear it. I guess we can go, then."

Grant knew he had to debrief her, ask for all the details of her abduction and captivity and get all he could on the kidnapper before sending her home. But he'd have to do that somewhere else and later, when she'd calmed down a little. Maybe after her meltdown.

Who knew when that would happen? Soon, he expected. He knew from experience that the higher the adrenalin level, the harder one fell. The inquisition could wait awhile.

He hated debriefing. Extraction of a hostage or victim was his thing; the rest of the job package, a necessary evil.

Grant had to smile. Marie Beauclair hadn't waited for a rescue. Spunky little devil had really saved herself. If he hadn't been there, poised to make entry when he saw her coming out of that window, she'd probably have found help somewhere in the village and gotten back to Munich on her own.

Unless she'd been caught in the back alleys or on a deserted street. The thought sent a chill up his spine. At least he'd quickly gotten her away from the scene, as ordered.

That probably accounted for the smidgeon of thankfulness he saw in her eyes. The mistrust—he couldn't figure it, unless she now feared men in general. Not that unusual, he supposed, given what she'd just been through.

He should reassure her that he was only there to take care of her and keep her safe. "You'll be all right now," he said, reaching out to take her arm.

She moved back before he could touch her. "I know. And I don't need babying, so knock it off."

"Your feet…" he reminded her.

"My feet are just fine. If I fall down, you can pick me up, okay?"

"Okay," he agreed with a sigh, "Miss Independent."

She shot him a glare that would curdle milk and stalked out the doors ahead of him. Testy little thing, but he chalked that up to her ordeal and didn't blame her a bit.

That made him wonder what she was like before. Soft as silk, he'd bet. He knew her type. He could almost picture her attending consulate functions in a slinky little black dress, that cloud of hair done up on top of her head, natural-looking makeup that took hours to apply. And killer stilettos on those pretty little feet.

He glanced at her hands. She had the badly chipped remnants of a French manicure, and her wrists looked raw. His lips tightened in anger at the bastard who'd tied her up and scared her to death.

"Don't be afraid he'll find you," Grant told her. "We'll see that you're safe."

She gave a short cough of disbelief as she stopped in her tracks and narrowed those wide blue eyes. "He damn well better be afraid I'll find *him!*"

Grant shook his head and suppressed a smile. "Get in the car, tiger."

He couldn't help feeling sorry for Marie. She'd had a horrible experience, and he thought the exam at the hospital hadn't been any fun, either. Even though she hadn't been raped, he knew how violated she felt.

He had believed her determined bravado was beginning to fade when she'd gotten a bit teary and pleaded with him to go by her apartment. He was afraid just being where she was abducted would set her off, but she seemed to need that ring she mentioned. Maybe that symbolized some small victory over the kidnapper, that he hadn't found it or taken it from her.

When they arrived in Munich, Marie gave Grant directions to her apartment, a second-floor walk-up in a German neighborhood near the consulate.

They stopped at the super's flat and got a key. The old man was inordinately glad to see her, apologizing profusely for the fact that someone might have copied his keys and stolen access to her flat from him.

Grant noted that Beauclair spoke excellent Deutsch and conversed easily with the man as she reassured him he'd done nothing wrong. She looked to Grant for backup.

"The report said the lock showed signs of tampering," Grant told him. "The man was a professional. No one's holding you responsible, Herr Horst."

Marie thanked Grant with a perfunctory nod and a smile, shook the super's hand and headed upstairs. No hesitation, he noted. She didn't seem afraid to return to the kidnap scene.

"Where'd you learn German?" Grant asked as they climbed the stairs.

"A retired teacher, a neighbor and friend. She was fluent in several languages and began teaching me early on. She said it might help me land a job when I grew up, and she was right. I had an ear for it, my memory made it easy, and we both enjoyed it."

"Lucky you. I lived over here for several years and still had to suffer through language school to get it right."

"Defense Language Institute at the Presidio?"

"Yeah. You ever been there?" he asked.

"Nope, just heard about it. I haven't traveled much yet, even over here. I planned to. That's one of the primary reasons I volunteered for the position, but they've kept me too busy since I arrived."

She stood back as he unlocked the door for her and went in first to check things out.

He liked that she was prudent enough to let him do that. However, she didn't seem at all leery about entering the apartment. Brave of her, or else she was a damn good actress.

Lights worked, so the utilities were still on. Investigators had obviously finished with the place. A few boxes were stacked in the middle of the room. Someone had packed her personal items but hadn't shipped them yet. It didn't appear that she had very much.

He continued into the bedroom, and there were a few more boxes. The bathroom was empty of her toiletries and towels and shone from a recent cleaning.

"All clear," he said, then realized as he turned that she was standing right behind him. She looked like a lost little waif, so tiny in his sweats and socks, hands clasped in front of her.

Her expression had altered considerably, and he figured this wide-eyed trepidation was her real reaction to the place. "It's okay," he said, gently touching her shoulder. "There's no one here but us."

"Thank goodness." Her words were breathy, almost a whisper, as if she uttered them reluctantly.

"Hey, why don't you call your family and talk to them? Mercier will have notified them by now that you're safe, but maybe you'd like to tell them yourself. A familiar voice might make you feel better."

She bit her bottom lip and avoided his questioning gaze. "Maybe later. After a shower."

She stepped past him, approached the boxes and peeled the packing tape off one. "Towel," she muttered, withdrew one and draped it over her shoulder. He watched as she opened another container and fished out a pair of jeans and a pullover. And undies. Beige lace. Brief.

He cleared his throat and looked away. "I'll, uh, just leave you to take your shower."

"Thanks…Grant," she replied, using his given name for the first time. Why that seemed significant puzzled him. She wasn't flirting, more as if she was earnestly reaching out, needing a friend.

He could understand why she felt friendless. Her people hadn't sent anyone to save her. Her family couldn't ransom her. He wondered if she had a significant other who was just sitting on his butt back there in the States, waiting for a miracle or word of her death.

Well, that wasn't his problem, Grant thought. He

would take good care of her as long as she was in his custody, of course, and until he saw her off, he'd be her friend if she needed one. No risk there.

There had been a time when he did consider making friends a risk. For one thing, they had always moved away or he had. A lasting relationship of any kind had been his greatest wish when he was young, but he soon learned that short-term was his best bet. No gut-wrenching goodbyes to suffer.

Whenever he did get involved with people, he felt responsible for them, compelled to look after them, fix what was wrong with them, ease their way in life however he could. And then they would have to move on, or he would, leaving behind a feeling of distress on his part that they were going off on their own and might be unable to cope. Yeah, it was definitely better not to let himself care all that much.

Because he soon realized that was a cold attitude to live with, he had adopted a smiling, good-ol'-boy warmth that put people at ease. That way, they'd be less aware that he kept a safe emotional distance. He'd had to do that with the people under his command or he would have gone crazy.

He did much better with this civilian job. Working alone sure had its advantages. In this particular case, he was relieved that his association with Marie Beauclair would be temporary.

Grant went into the living room and clicked on the television to cover the sound of her shower. He didn't want to imagine her wet and naked. It just didn't feel right to do that. But he couldn't seem to help it.

Given what she had endured, his response filled him with guilt. He concentrated on pity, a much safer reaction to her and a lot more appropriate. Poor little thing.

Twenty minutes into a boring old movie, Grant began to get worried. The shower was still running. The water should be stone-cold by this time.

Was she in there, crying? Had she gone to sleep? Drowned herself? He'd better check.

"Ms. Beauclair?" He knocked several times. "You okay?" He knocked again. "*Marie*? Answer me right now or I'm coming in."

Nothing.

Grant tried the handle. Locked. Well, there was no window in the bathroom, so he knew she hadn't climbed out. Either she had passed out or was unable to speak for some reason. He backed up and ran against the door. And promptly bounced off. Dammit, he'd break his shoulder. He shouted again. No answer.

Chapter 3

Grant reached in his pocket and pulled out his pick tools. It took a minute or so to slip the mechanism on the bathroom door and unlock it. The room was filled with steam, but a quick scan showed it was empty.

She had thumbed the lock and pulled it shut to buy some time. But how had she gotten past him?

Grant turned off the water and went back into the bedroom. He raked back the draperies and cursed. The window at the back of the building was open. The thin line of a rappelling rope anchored to the bed frame snaked out one edge of the window and dangled nearly to the ground. Probably kept as a means of fire escape. Why hadn't he thought of that?

He ran a hand through his hair and gave it a tug.

Tricked like the greenest recruit, but how the hell was he to guess she'd even want to take off on her own? Where the hell did she think she was going?

After her kidnapper, of course. And the logical place for her to start would be back at that little burg where she'd been held.

A foot-long section of baseboard near the closet lay loose on the floor. The cavity that had lain behind it was the hidey-hole for the grandmother's ring, if there had even been one, and whatever else she'd felt compelled to conceal so carefully.

He knew exactly what that would be. If he were her, working undercover, he would have his real I.D. and creds stashed somewhere safe. That, and cash.

Always have a back door. Her fire-escape rope verified she'd had that. He was a little paranoid himself about any abode with only one exit, so he couldn't fault her for that. He could, however, curse her for using it in this instance.

He pulled out his phone and called Mercier. Embarrassing as it was, he would have to report this snafu to control and take his lumps for it. He was mad as hell with the sneaky little devil. And sort of impressed in spite of that.

Mercier wasn't impressed at all, especially with him. Grant could almost see the boss rolling his eyes.

"I know where she went," Grant declared. "She tried to convince me to let her help catch her abductor. Since I said no, in no uncertain terms, she's gone off on her own. I'll have her on the plane within twenty-four hours."

"No," Mercier said. "If she's that gung ho and that

quick on her feet, let her help. You say she's seen him and heard him. Catch up with her and see how she does."

"Jack, she'll just slow me down. I'd rather do this by myself."

"Noted, but indulge me." An order, not a request.

"All right, but if she gets in the way, I'm sending her back, cuffed if necessary!"

"If you have to," Mercier agreed. "Give her a chance, though. She's been a real asset to the Company, had as much training as you and obviously has had real initiative. No reason to treat her as a novice."

Yeah. No reason at all. Except that Grant really didn't think she was up to this. He realized his take on it was colored by his personal opinions. As politically incorrect and chauvinistic as those might be, they were grounded in experience.

His mother had given every outward appearance of strength and courage. Everyone had always commented on how well she coped. Only Grant had known her to break down when no one else could see or hear. One of his first memories was that of sitting in the hallway outside her bedroom door, holding the little stuffed dog she had made for him, feeling her fright and wondering how to comfort her. His dad was overseas where they couldn't go that time, and his mom couldn't handle it. Her pretense left a lasting impression on him.

And so had Betty Schonrock, the girl who had everything. Everything but someone to watch out for her and care what happened to her. God, would he live with that failure forever? Twenty years had passed and it still troubled him. It hadn't been his place to protect her and what else could he have done? He ought to let it go.

He fully understood that women wanted and truly tried to be as strong as men. Maybe some were. He just didn't think this one was as self-sufficient as she thought she was.

Marie Beauclair looked incredibly fragile and down-right helpless at times. Okay, but while he knew that part of that had been an act to throw him off guard, her tears had been real enough. Her fear, the trembling and pain hadn't been faked. At least he didn't think so. Had they?

He had never worked with a female partner. He'd even caught himself worrying about the female agents employed by COMPASS. They seemed capable and got the job done, so he heard. But in his opinion, women were just more sensitive, more vulnerable, and they should be protected, not thrown into situations where they might be hurt.

They were physically weaker, a proven fact. And while they were probably more tolerant to pain than men were, he couldn't see any justification for exposing them to it intentionally. Participating in an investigation of her own abduction and imprisonment surely qualified as painful where Marie was concerned. Dangerous, too.

Grant pocketed his phone and started after her. Maybe if he hurried, he could beat her there.

Marie sailed down the autobahn, grinning at the speed of her little Audi roadster. She loved the convertible, the one fancy she did love about her cover as an eager young admin assistant with her first international job. She had to admit she liked the clothes, too. Had to dress to impress!

No need for that today, though. Her small duffel was packed with only practical stuff, not the froufrou. She wore dark jeans, a black knit shirt and black running shoes with thick socks to cushion her cuts. Her braid kept her still-wet hair slicked back for the most part, but as it dried the wind grabbed at tendrils around her face.

The little Glock 27 lay on the seat beside her, ready to tuck into her belt when she got back to the scene. Dressed to kill, she thought with a smile.

Hopefully the kidnapper would be out looking for her in the village still, thinking he'd find her wandering around the streets half naked, begging for help or curled up in an alley nearby, hiding. With any luck, she'd find him first.

She imagined trussing him up, strapping him to the hood of her car like a hunting kill and hauling him to the nearest Polizei station. He had definitely picked the wrong victim this time.

Was Grant Tyndal still sitting in front of her television, or had he caught on by now? Poor guy, never had a clue. Eyelash fluttering and lip trembling went a long way with him. Pity it had taken *her* so many years to discover the power of that—she might have saved herself a boatload of angst early on.

She felt sorry for Tyndal, but he could have cut her a little slack and agreed to let her assist. Despite his periodic gruffness, he had been a real softie and easy to dupe. He seemed an all right guy, at least on the surface, so she hoped he didn't get into too much trouble for losing her.

This probably canceled any chance of her working for COMPASS, but so what? She liked the job she had.

She had been procrastinating on a response to the offer anyway. It would be an excellent move professionally, she was flattered they wanted her and she probably would have accepted. But the European assignment had been really exciting so far and she hated to give it up so soon.

The Company would reassign her to another post, and she'd carry on, attending parties, searching, listening and mentally recording, playing the featherbrained innocent overawed by the powerful who surrounded her.

In what seemed no time at all, Marie reached the exit leading to the village where she'd been stashed. When she got to the town, she slowed and parked on the sidewalk in front of a small row of shops.

She slipped her weapon into the back of her belt, pulled her shirttail down over it and got out to join them.

The village was a bit larger than she reckoned, and it took a while to locate the building from which she'd escaped.

The alley adjacent to the building was deserted. Marie walked around to the entrance. The door was unlocked, even standing open a little. She pulled her weapon, hesitated, listened and heard nothing. Quietly, she edged it open a little more and slipped inside.

It was fairly dark, dank smelling and apparently empty. There was a chair, a bare cot and a table near a door to what she figured must be her former cell. That door, too, was cracked open a few inches.

Carefully, she approached, gun out and off safety. She kicked it fully open and shouted, "Polizei!"

"Bang. You're dead," a quiet voice declared in English. He sat, hands linked over his stomach, leaning back against the wall in the same straight chair she'd used to break the window.

"Dammit, Tyndal! I almost shot you!" She lowered her weapon and shook her head. "How'd you get here before I did?"

"Shortcut," he drawled. "What took you so long?"

"What do you mean? I flew!"

He rocked forward and got up. "Not fast enough, either of us. Our boy's gone already. I just found this in the other room, though." He held out a scrap of paper with a few words scribbled on it. "It's in Dutch, I think."

She examined the paper. "Yeah, it's a supply list. So he's probably either from the Netherlands or had Dutch parents. That must be his mother tongue. He used it to make a list, and I heard him curse in it. Not much of a clue to his whereabouts now, though."

"It's all we have so far."

Marie looked up at him and grinned. "Did you just say *we?*"

He shrugged and nodded, looking resigned.

"Not your decision, I take it?"

He shook his head. "Mercier said to watch you. So, show me what you got. If it's good enough, I guess you get the job."

"I have a job right now—getting this guy. One thing bothers me. If he intended for me to escape, maybe he meant for the authorities to find that," she said, staring at the paper as she spoke.

"You think he let you go?"

"Sure made it easy enough. And he let me overhear him speaking in Dutch."

"Let you, huh? Maybe he thought you were still out from the drugs. I don't think we can assume—"

Marie interrupted. "So what do you think? False leads?"

"I don't know. I found the paper right before I heard you coming and haven't had time to examine it. Give me a minute." He turned away, holding the scrap between his palms.

It was a full minute before he answered. "No. He took something out of his pocket, dropped this accidentally."

Marie didn't appreciate the humor, but she laughed anyway. "Thanks, oh, great swami. Did you divine anything else?"

Oddly enough, he didn't laugh with her. "I'm psychic."

"Well, excuse me for not recognizing that. Your ears aren't pointy like Mr. Spock's."

"A skeptic. Well, at least my luck's consistent today."

"You're serious," she guessed. "You really think you can…"

"I really *know* I can, and I don't intend to debate it with you right now. I thought maybe since you have a photographic memory—something very few people possess and some consider strange—that you'd at least have an open mind about it."

"That's why COMPASS wants me? So all that stuff about the team having unique powers isn't just some outlandish rumor?"

"Hardly. But it's not up to me to convince you. Mercier can do that if you come on board. If not, it's just as well you retain your disbelief. We don't need it advertised."

She cocked her head and pursed her lips. "So, how's it work? Your gift, I mean. And how *well* does it work?"

If she expected defensiveness, she didn't get it. He pocketed the paper and answered matter-of-factly, "Only works with touching things, not people, which we figure might be an early developed defense mechanism on my part. Or it could simply be a limitation. Accuracy's about 80 percent in my case."

"Oh, so you admit that sometimes it doesn't work?" she asked politely.

He nodded. "It depends on how much energy was expended on the object that was held or used and for how long it was exposed. Our boy obviously put some thought into making the list. Got more than I figured from it."

"Okay, let's hear it. What did you *get?*" She asked, humoring him while trying not to view him as a crazy she ought to run from.

After a pause, Tyndal added almost reluctantly, "He's working for somebody else."

Marie avoided his eyes and gave a succinct nod, not wanting to make him angry by questioning this ability. Psychic mumbo jumbo aside, he had access to a number of enforcement agencies and therefore more resources for investigating this than she had.

She needed him, crazy or not. Now how could she make him need *her?*

Chapter 4

"If I give you a picture of him," Marie offered, "you could have it run through Interpol?"

"Sure, but how—"

"Art major. Worked my way through LSU doing sidewalk portraits around Jackson Square."

"That's not in your file."

"Don't tell the IRS. I worked for cash only. I'll need charcoal and a sketch pad."

She pushed past him and returned to the outer room. Have you checked out the rest of this place. Maybe he dropped something else."

He followed. "Because of you, we have breaks in the case now, you furnishing that likeness of the perp and this, the location where he held you. None of the others that lived have been able to provide any information. They were drugged the entire time, then dumped in a public park, either alive or dead. Forensics hasn't gotten anything, either, but this time, we've lucked out.

"I got a partial print off the bed frame."

Marie smiled her approval. "You brought a print kit?"

"Boy Scout. Always prepared." He held up the salute.

"Hey, I hear they give *badges* for that!"

"Funny girl." He ushered her through the door to the street. "You aren't always this perky, are you? I hope this is another guise to throw me off the real you. Perky just irritates the hell out of me."

"And condescension annoys me, just so you know. Your car or mine?"

"Mine. All my gear is in it and your ride isn't exactly low profile. Is that hot little number part of your fluffy persona, or are you naturally a show-off?"

"You saw my car? When?"

"No, I haven't seen it, but I did read your file. Except for your art and erstwhile tax evasion, I know just about everything there is to know about you."

She raised her eyebrows and gave him a tight-lipped smile. "Believe that at your own risk."

He guided her to the same gray sedan they'd used earlier. The car looked as if it had seen its better days in the last century. It wasn't a pretty ride like hers, but it had made great time this morning and had beaten her here on the return trip. Hidden power beneath the hood. Like the driver, maybe?

Marie made a face as he opened the passenger door for her. She stepped away from his touch when he tried to usher her inside. "You really are a Boy Scout, Tyndal. Help little old ladies across the street, too?"

"Whether they want to go or not," he said, making her laugh.

She liked the man in spite of herself. He didn't like her much, though. Thought she was deceptive, impulsive and too aggressive. She didn't have to be psychic to get that. She also didn't need extrasensory perception to know he was physically interested, though he hid it pretty well. She could use that. Sometimes it was the most valuable tool available, but it was risky and she seldom employed it.

Her touch-me-not attitude was for real, but most men saw it only as a come on. It must intrigue them or something. With Tyndal, that would probably work very well. She needed him on her side, helping her but not coming on to her. That last part bothered her.

Unless she had misjudged him, he wouldn't make any sexual demands, because of his ethics. Not that she trusted any man's ethics very far. There was a price to pay for following through with a calculated flirtation, a very heavy price she was not willing to pay again.

But fantasies didn't cost anything, she thought with a sigh. Fantasy was always better than the reality anyway.

"Pull around to the main drag," she ordered as he got behind the wheel. "There's a stationer, where they might sell art supplies. If not, I can make do with plain paper and a pencil. While I shop for that, you can call for somebody to pick up my vehicle and store it."

He did precisely as she instructed, which Marie took as a sign that he was prudent. She didn't, however, mistake it for submission on his part. He still thought he was running this show and she would let him think it. For now.

She worked best on her own and resented the fact that she needed him. She didn't like needing anyone for anything. Surviving on her own was a way of life for her. Lonely at times, but that was no excuse for abandoning what worked best. But partnering on this mission was necessary.

Grant cast sideways glances at the sketchbook as he drove. She was damn good. "We have another artist on the team, Renee Alexander. You'll like her."

"Assuming I ever meet her. Is this all she does?"

"No," he said. "She's an agent."

"That's not what I meant. Can she do what you said you could do? You know, psychic stuff?"

"Some." He didn't expound on it, since Marie wasn't on board with the team yet. He'd probably volunteered more than he ought to already.

She got the message and didn't ask anything else about it. Grant liked that she sensed when to drop things without being told.

Her drawing looked almost finished when he pulled off the autobahn an hour later to fill the gas tank and get some food. She hadn't eaten a decent meal yet and it was already three o'clock.

"You must be starved," he commented. "What would you like?"

"Fast food. Hamburger," she muttered, still intent on her drawing.

"C'mon. That stuff will kill you. Let's get a schnitzel."

"Oh, yeah, like that will keep your arteries clear. Humor me and find some Golden Arches, will you? And a beer. I want beer and a burger." She rubbed the picture with one finger, smudging in a shadow. "Make that two. Two burgers. One beer, unless you're driving all the way. Then I'll have two of each."

Grant clicked his tongue, exasperated. "How *do* you keep that figure?"

"I only indulge when I've been kidnapped," she said with a smile that looked forced. "Buy me some comfort?"

He bought her some comfort, watching her with no little fascination as she consumed two quarter-pounders with cheese, fries with mayonnaise and two cups of draft.

"Isn't it wild that you can buy beer everywhere? Even here?" she asked.

"I see you're still going through culture shock. Do you even *like* beer?"

She wrinkled her nose. "Unfortunately, I do. German beer anyway."

"Apple pie?" he asked, nudging one toward her side of the table and wondering just how much she could hold in that tiny frame before exploding.

She took the pie and simply looked at the cardboard container longingly. "Maybe later."

"Maybe? No maybe about it, you eat like a lumber-jack," he said with a laugh.

"I haven't had a hamburger or pie since I was a kid," she admitted. "I had to give 'em up." She shook her head as if she couldn't believe what she'd just eaten. Her gaze met his. "Aren't you going to ask me why?"

"Okay, why?"

"I was a fat kid." Her blue eyes widened in that engaging way she had, and she nodded for emphasis. "Really, *really* fat."

And now she was really, really tipsy. "Yeah? How long since you had beer?"

"Month or so. I love the taste of it but don't indulge a lot. I'm not much of a drinker."

Obviously. Her eyelids were drooping.

The stress was catching up with her, adrenalin crashing right on top of those two little cups of beer. "I think you need a nap. Let's go and you can sleep on the way."

"Wait! You have to get the picture to Interpol!"

"Is it finished? Let's have a look." He pulled the sketchbook to his side of the table and opened the cover.

The profile was detailed, right down to the mole near the eye and stubble on the jaw and neck. Off in one corner was a man's left hand with a scar delineated on the wrist. "Man, it's so realistic! You *are* good."

"Photographic. That's what I do best," she replied.

He pulled out his cell phone, caught the images on his screen, then e-mailed them along with a short message to Mercier, who would do the proper distribution. "There. All done."

Grant smoothed the page down with his hand and almost gasped. The energy radiating from the drawing virtually leaped up his arm. *Rage. Determination. And suppressed fear.*

Damn. He couldn't let her go into this with that much emotion. It would wreck the whole mission, not to mention what it might do to *her* if she ever actually confronted her captor. But now was not the time to discuss it.

She wouldn't voluntarily rescue herself, not easily anyway. Maybe he could somehow make her see reason before they reached Holland.

He led her to the car and settled her in the backseat, stuffing his folded jacket under her head as a pillow.

Grant had noticed how she shied away from him, but now she accepted his help easily enough. Either she trusted him a bit more or the beer had lowered her defenses. Any woman who had undergone all that she had in the last twenty-four hours probably couldn't stand any man getting too close. From now on, he'd keep contact to a minimum whenever possible.

A shame, he thought, as his fingers brushed against her braid. She needed hugging in the worst way and didn't even know it.

"Thanks," she mumbled, cradling her face in one hand and closing her eyes.

"Fat little kid, huh?" he muttered to himself as he closed the door and went around to the driver's side and got in. "You sure fixed that problem."

She was as slender as she could be without looking skinny now, and he suspected the curves she did have were mostly muscle. No doubt she worked out regularly. Excellent shape. His admiration for her kicked up another notch now that he knew she wasn't just born with lucky genes.

"I was skinny," he said, his voice hushed in pretend conversation with his sleeping passenger. "Tall and a beanpole. Geeky, to boot. I know what it takes to shape up and how miserable it can be doing it. Good for you, babe."

He thought he heard a sleepy chuckle from the back-seat but decided he must have imagined it. She was dead to the world back there.

Grant smiled to himself, trying to picture Marie as a roly-poly adolescent. All he could see in his mind were those remarkably expressive delft-blue eyes, bright with enthusiasm, intelligence and all-consuming energy.

He hated to disappoint her by sending her home. Maybe Mercier would know what to do with her, because he sure as hell didn't.

They were already halfway to Holland from Munich, and Frankfurt was out of the way. He'd take her on to Amsterdam and put her on a plane. Then he could get down to business with no distractions.

Marie sensed that in her temporarily vulnerable state she'd given away too much about herself in her effort to befriend Tyndal. He had identified with her childhood problem. She'd figured he would do that. Didn't all kids have socialization problems of one kind or another? But she had laid it out all wrong, and now he probably saw her as defensive, compensatory and a little out of control. He would dump her if she gave him the chance.

She wasn't drunk on two beers—not by a long stretch—but the beer had loosened her up while she was winding down from the high of all the excitement and exhaustion.

No use regretting her dietary lapse or trying to get too

close to him too soon. She made it a point never to second-guess her decisions or actions. Counterproductive.

Doing something was almost always better than doing nothing at all. Her policy was to go for broke, roll with the consequences, good or bad, and try to make them work for her. Right now she needed sleep, but she couldn't afford to let this slide.

With that in mind, she sat up and leaned on the back of the front seat. "Why do you think he let me get away? I'd like your take on it."

"You seriously think he *let* you?" Tyndal glanced at her in the rearview mirror.

"It didn't occur to me at the time, but in retrospect, it seems he made it pretty easy. He was speaking Dutch and talking pretty loudly. Could be that he was trying to establish that the abductions are not terrorist acts but simple kidnappings. As a witness who got away, I could send the investigation in a different direction. That would explain why he gave me the opportunity to run."

"Could be. But I think the abductions *are* terrorist acts. The earmarks are there. American victims from American embassies and consulates, huge ransoms."

He glanced up at her again, meeting her eyes in the rearview mirror. "Think about this: He didn't know you were a trained agent. And he couldn't have known how long that drug would affect you or precisely how soon you'd be able to overhear him. How would he know you'd even recognize Dutch when you heard it?"

Marie considered that. "Then why did he make it so easy for me to get away?"

"It would *not* have been easy for most people. If you

were the little clerk he thought you were, you'd probably still be there. Now why don't you get some rest?
You've got to be wiped out."

She sighed. "Okay, but I'm fine, just so you know.
You really think he's gone to Holland?"

"Yes. Amsterdam."

"Explain. The vibe you picked up from that piece of
paper?"

"Something like that. Don't want to bore you with
details you wouldn't believe anyway."

He took a deep breath and released it, firming his
hands on the steering wheel as he looked in the rearview
mirror again. "You need to go home, Marie. It's the
best thing all around, for you and for the investigation."

"I don't think you want me to work this by myself."

"I don't want you to work this *at all*. You'd like to
kill him, Marie. Don't deny it."

Well, he had her there. "Wouldn't you?" she asked,
sincerely curious. "The bastard grabbed me in my own
kitchen, drugged me and tied me up like an express
package! Of course I'd like to get back at him in the
worst way. But I won't go in like Rambo and kill him
and any chance of finding out why he did it or who's
running the show." She pouted for a second. "Give me
a little credit for control."

Tyndal remained quiet. Was he thinking that over or
just refusing to discuss it?

"Well?" she prompted.

He shifted in his seat, body language broadcasting
that his decision was highly reluctant. "All right. But
only because Mercier wants you evaluated. One screw-

up and I'll have the locals haul you in and hold you for me as a material witness. Got that?"

"Got it." And she had, precisely what she wanted. "Now I think I'll take your advice and get some shut-eye unless you need me to drive."

"Get real. Go to sleep, Marie."

She lay down and closed her eyes, satisfied she'd handled him exactly right. Maybe she should have questioned him a bit more on the psychic thing, but that could wait. He obviously believed he'd gotten something using his psychic powers, and arguing wouldn't change a thing.

At least driving to Amsterdam gave them something to do while they waited for a possible I.D. to come back from Interpol. But somehow it all seemed too convenient.

Maybe identifying the print or the sketch would send them in the right direction if this one was wrong. You ran with what you had, and right now all she had was Tyndal and his *woo-woo* touch.

She drifted off, thinking about those hands of his....

Chapter 5

Grant drove on, waking her only when they crossed the border to show their passports and visas. It turned into a big deal when he declared their weapons and presented credentials. Several phone calls later and they were again on their way, properly vetted. He was used to the hassle and glad to see the border guards were doing their job.

Marie promptly went back to sleep. He phoned Mercier and reported, then called ahead and made a reservation. When they reached Amsterdam, it was late evening.

"Hey, sleepyhead, we're here." The city was beautiful at night, with lights reflecting off the canals from centuries-old buildings. There was a warmth and timelessness about it. "This is one of my favorite places."

"New one for me. I always wanted to come here but never had the opportunity." She had popped up from the backseat and leaned forward. "Impressive. Where are we staying?"

"I called ahead and made reservations while you were asleep. We'll be sharing a room."

She was totally silent for way too long. Then she answered. "Absolutely not."

"Look, if you're worried that I'm desperately seeking sex, forget it. We're partners, however temporary that might be, so it's out of the question. I figured it might make you nervous to be alone tonight."

He wondered if she'd realize he had another reason.

"And if we share a room, you won't have to worry about me climbing out a window and disappearing," she guessed.

"There is that," he admitted. "C'mon, I swear not to leave the toilet seat up or accost you in your sleep. Scout's honor."

She rested her chin on her folded arms, and he couldn't quite see her face as she answered. "You've seen me at my absolute worst, so I can't think you'd even be interested after that. Still, it's not a good idea to share a room."

Yeah, well, that was probably true, since he was *definitely interested*. But rather than worry her with that admission, he changed the subject.

"Look, there's something I haven't mentioned. I'm pretty sure I know where he's staying."

"The kidnapper? How could you possibly know that?"

"A feeling. A word that popped into my head when

I was zoned in on the list." Grant knew she didn't believe, and he knew he could be wrong. But that word had struck a resounding note that wouldn't fade. "It's more than a hunch. I think he's at the Zuider."

"Is that a hotel?"

"Yeah. It's a small place near the red-light district. You and I won't stay there, of course. He might see and recognize you, but I would like to be within walking distance of it. I decided on the Pulitzer, but they only had one room available."

"My goodness, how convenient was that! Pardon my simplicity, but here's an idea—why don't you simply go to his hotel, find out which room he's in and arrest him?"

"Because we don't know his real name or the one he's using."

"We have his picture," she argued.

"I know, but we have no jurisdiction at the moment. Hopefully we'll get some results on the sketch and print tomorrow. Soon as we have that, we'll bring the locals in on it, get vetted and proceed from there. Maybe if we just keep tabs on him, he'll lead us to the one who hired him."

"So meanwhile, we go to your Pulitzer prize hotel and shack up. That's your plan?"

He smiled. "No. We go the Pulitzer and cohabit like partnering agents. Strictly platonic, so relax. In addition to its location, it has all the modern amenities along with charm and quaintness. You'll love it, trust me."

They entered the seventeenth-century group of houses that had been converted into a hotel. Grant held the door for her and was surprised that she let him, because she was so independent.

He shook his head as she swept past him. Why couldn't women these days realize that deference to them was hardwired in some men, inborn, automatic and almost impossible to reverse? His dad had drummed it in right along with all the other values he felt necessary.

What was the matter with her anyway? Maybe she thought he didn't notice those quick little glances of suspicion every time he gestured for her to go first, gave her a compliment or did anything to help her. She must suspect him of some ulterior motive, such as maybe he was trying to seduce her by playing the gentleman.

Well, he guessed he couldn't blame her. She'd probably been hit on a lot, pretty as she was. That must cause her to look at any nice gesture as one she'd be expected to repay.

They needed to talk about it so he could set her straight, but he figured she didn't need another confrontation right now. Surely she trusted him a little, since she had agreed finally to stay in the same room. He wanted her to feel safe and comfortable with that.

Had trying to please her become almost as important as the mission? Grant knew only that he'd definitely had her in mind when he decided where to stay and had chosen a place he thought she would enjoy.

"Not too shabby," she commented when they entered their room. She tossed her purse and small shoulder tote onto one of the double beds and went over to the window. "Great view of the canal. Look! It's so pretty as far as you can see. I'll bet it's been just like this for centuries."

"Thought you'd like it. Want to go out and walk for a bit?"

She did. They freshened up and went back down to find a place serving a late dinner and do a walk-by of the Zuider. If she was still ill at ease about sharing accommodations, she didn't show it.

"More comfort food?" he asked as they strolled along the canal. He had an almost overwhelming urge to take her hand but didn't do so.

She shook her head. "Can't afford to indulge twice in one day. Something light would be better."

Grant pointed to a small café, and they walked toward it. On the way he caught sight of their side-by-side reflections in the plate-glass window and a pang of longing struck him at the sight. A couple, yet not a couple.

They looked well matched and had a great deal in common. He felt something for Marie that he couldn't quite define, a sort of connection probably borne of grudging respect and physical attraction combined with the urge to protect.

She had shot down all the qualms he had about becoming friends. Just like that, she had sneaked under his guard and he'd dropped his hard-and-fast rule of no emotional attachment. He really wanted to be friends. And more.

He wouldn't act on that last urge, however. He didn't need the professional problems that would surely result, and besides, he had promised her.

She looked up at him as he reached to open the door for her, and she smiled as if she'd read his thoughts and was thanking him. No suspicion in that look, only trust.

As thunderbolts went, the one that hit him then shook him to the core.

His father had experienced the same thing and Grant had heard the story time and again, told proudly, too. Love at first sight. Oh, man.

He remembered thinking how ridiculous it was, how unlike his dad who never made snap decisions, who considered every angle, every possible consequence. Now Grant got it. In spades.

In that one dizzying instant, he realized she was the one. And there wasn't a damn thing he could do about it.

Talk about a rock and a hard place....

Marie hadn't seriously objected to sharing the room with Tyndal. She wouldn't sleep anyway. In the first place, she'd slept earlier in the day. Wide-awake and with access to the top-of-the-line laptop he'd brought with him, she'd keep herself busy.

Even if they had stayed in the same hotel the kidnapper was supposed to be in, she wasn't worried about him seeing her. The man was probably hundreds of miles away from Amsterdam anyway. Grant's delusions were just that, but she'd humor him and keep him happy.

Once they had a name to go with the face she had seen, things would heat up and they'd probably take off for another country altogether.

The kidnapper could have gone anywhere. If he happened to be a known terrorist suspect, they'd probably get info on the latest sightings. It was hard to hide for long when the powers that be decided to keep a close eye on you.

She'd had her shower, had pulled on the knit shorts and T-shirt she'd brought from her apartment to sleep in, and was sitting cross-legged in the middle of her bed, surfing on the laptop.

Grant exited the bathroom, rubbing a towel over his head. He wore shorts, gray ones, brief ones. His chest was bare, well muscled and dusted with dark hair. His legs were phenomenal, she noted. Then she tried to dismiss the overall impression from her mind. Okay, so he had a fantastic body. It wasn't the first one she'd seen, and it wouldn't be the last.

"Find anything interesting?" he asked.

"Maps."

"Memorizing them?" he asked, plopping down on the bed next to hers.

"Will this keep you awake?"

"Not at all. See what you can find on the Zuider."

He seemed so convinced the guy was there that he wouldn't listen to her if she objected. "Anything else you can think of for me to look up?"

"Nope. Well, have at it. I'm bushed." With that, he tossed the towel aside, stood, yanked back the coverlet and crawled into his bed.

She tried not to watch. It seemed too intimate a thing. It had been years since she'd seen a man simply go to bed. And even then, it hadn't been like this. Comfy, yet uncomfortable. Sexless, yet arousing.

He wrestled his pillow into shape and, with one arm beneath it, settled on his side with his back to her and sighed. Marie held her breath. Was that it?

"Good night," he mumbled. Within sixty seconds, his breathing had slowed and evened out.

She almost laughed. Nobody went to sleep that easily. She continued to watch, but he never moved. If he was faking, it must take quite an effort.

Show-off—that's what he was. *Look at me. I'm trained to grab sleep wherever and whenever.*

Marie shook her head and focused again on the laptop, determined to ignore him and his bare, lightly tanned back and shoulders.

After a while she was able to stop stealing glances. Her eyelids grew heavy, and her own back protested her position. Too bad, she thought, but there wasn't a man alive she trusted enough to actually sleep with in the same room.

He thought she was afraid of him as a man, and she was. Sex on its own didn't scare her; that wasn't it. It was what came after.

"You must *find* her!" Mamud Bahktar growled. "How is it that one simpleminded female outwits you? Have you hired imbeciles to do this, old man? You know where she lives, where her family lives. You have photographs of her. Find and kill her immediately!"

"It is not possible. She is gone, and they say there is no trace of her anywhere. No one reported her missing. Not one word about her turning up anywhere. We will take another immediately."

Mamud cursed in English, not blasphemy in his estimation. The American woman would have to die, to salve his pride if for no other reason. Even if she had grasped any information about the man who had taken her, it could never lead back to him or his cause.

However, the woman's escape threatened his double-edged plan to strike terror in the hearts of Americans serving overseas while also funding his special business venture in his own country. Those with whom he was to do that business would hear of it, and their trust in him would diminish if not evaporate.

"Find and kill her or you know what will happen next. This is not a request."

The rheumy voice cracked as it answered, "I tell you, she has not surfaced today and the hour is late. Surely something else happened to her after she got away or she would have sought help. She must be dead already or there would be an outcry of tremendous proportions considering the other abductions. Do not retaliate against me for this, Bahktar, or I will be of no further use to you." There was a slight hesitation before the threat. "And I will expose you. By name."

Mamud thought about that. He had no time to make other arrangements, and more ransoms were needed. The setup was too perfect to destroy it now, and that would serve nothing at this point.

"Fail me again and Fatima will die. Succeed with two more profitable targets and she may join you."

A heavy, rattling sigh. "Two more. Agreed."

"You will e-mail to me the scouting photographs and whatever financial information you can discover, just as you have done previously. We do not want any others with families too poor to afford the ransom."

"If possible," Shapur muttered.

"Do it. And hold on to the woman next time."

Chapter 6

Grant woke with a start. His eyes flew open, and he was instantly aware of everything around him. He hadn't lazed in a half-awake state since before he first joined the navy, and he sort of missed doing that sometimes. For example, this morning.

Nice hotel, sun beaming in the window, hot lady in the next bed. Yeah, it could be nice if the circumstances were a little different. The lady was over there and he was over here, for good reason.

He rolled over and the sight of her almost wrecked his resolve. Man, she looked inviting, even if it was inadvertent on her part.

She lay on her back, legs splayed a little, one arm curled beneath her head and the other flung out from the bed's edge. Somehow he'd expected her to sleep wound up in a tight little ball. She was such a bundle of energy that he'd hardly ever seen her relaxed. Grant took a moment to enjoy the view, then sighed and rolled out of bed.

"Up and at 'em, Beauclair!" he said in a loud voice. He didn't trust himself to get close enough to shake her awake. "Things to do, places to go, people to see!"

She groaned and rolled onto her side, opening one eye. Then she shot straight up in bed, both eyes wide and almost panicked.

He grabbed his shaving kit and headed for the bathroom, ignoring her shocked expression. Apparently, she'd forgotten where she was and had surprised herself by sleeping soundly.

Grant showered and shaved with the speed of light and was out in a few minutes. She ducked past him, her clothes in her hand and quickly shut the bathroom door.

Did she think he'd renege on his promise and jump her now? If he hadn't when she was lying sprawled out like a welcome mat, she was pretty damn safe. Maybe he should tell her that. Right, and get soundly slapped, he thought with a smile.

He dressed and checked his cell phone to see if it was juiced. They couldn't afford to miss a call from Mercier or Interpol. Grant focused on plans to bring in local law enforcement and was making notes on that when Marie came out of the bathroom.

Her gaze fell on the phone. "Did you get a call?"

"Not yet. With the time difference, I expect it will be a couple of hours." But even as the last word left his mouth, there was a knock on the door.

"Did you order room service?" Marie asked as she went to answer the knock. "Who is it?" she asked through the door.

"Karl Zahn with Interpol."

She opened the door and stood aside for him to enter, turning as she did to raise an eyebrow at Grant.

Zahn was thirtyish, balding and terminally pale. But he was polished to a fault in his three-piece suit, tasteful tie and spit-shined shoes. He carried an expensive, thin leather briefcase.

"Quick response," Grant said. "We were expecting a phone call." He greeted the man with a handshake. "Grant Tyndal with COMPASS. This is Marie Beauclair." He purposely didn't identify her affiliation with the CIA. As far as he knew, her cover was solidly intact and to be revealed only on a need-to-know basis.

Zahn nodded at Marie. "From the consulate in Munich, of course. Luck certainly was with you, Ms. Beauclair. I do hope you are recovering from your ordeal." His attitude was dismissive as he turned his attention immediately back to Grant.

Grant had to smile at Marie's dour expression. "I'm perfectly fine, and luck had very little to do with it," she declared.

Zahn paid no attention to that. Instead, he walked over to the small table by the window and opened his briefcase. "Let's get down to business, shall we?"

"Just tell us who we're dealing with," Grant said. "We can handle it from there."

Zahn spared another glance at Marie, then addressed Grant. "Perhaps we shouldn't involve the victim in this,

Agent Tyndal." He lowered his voice as if Marie were hard of hearing or too stupid to listen. "Women tend to get—"

"Trained occasionally and considered competent," Marie interrupted. "Don't let my size and blond hair fool you, and I promise not to let your lisp and condescending attitude affect my judgment of you."

"She did escape," Grant said with a wry grin. "All by herself."

Zahn dropped his gaze back to the briefcase, took a deep breath and released it with a nervous laugh. "Well, then, my mistake." He started to hand a folder to Grant, then swiveled a little and gave it to Marie with a bow of apology. "We identified the fellow almost immediately from the sketch, and the print confirmed it. He's been on our radar for some time. We suspect he was somehow involved with the murder of a filmmaker in The Hague, but there was no hard evidence. I'm sure you are both aware of the Islamic militant network operating in this country."

"The Hofstad Group," Grant affirmed.

Marie was reading the copy. "Says here they were plotting an attack on the intelligence service headquarters and members of Parliament." She looked up. "So now you believe they've extended their reach to the American embassies and consulates?"

"We can't know for certain if that's so," Zahn admitted, "only that this man might have worked for them at one time. We have very little background on him, as you see there." He pointed to the folder. "Perhaps he has family ties to the Middle East. We simply do not know his ethnicity, though his appearance is certainly suspect.

There are several names he uses, none verifiable as his true identity. He most frequently goes by Claude Onders."

"Do you know where he is now?" Grant asked.

"He was in Frankfurt fourteen days ago where he slipped surveillance. We kept an eye on his addresses there and here. He returned to Amsterdam late yesterday."

Marie was frowning down at the folder when she slowly raised her gaze to meet Grant's and said in a near whisper, "The Zuider Hotel! Grant, you—"

Grant held up a hand, hoping to silence her before she said more, but she had already stopped herself.

Zahn continued, missing the byplay completely. "I have already coordinated with the burgomaster and the chief prosecutor, who, of course, oversee police force activity. Your Special Agent Mercier has spoken with the chief commissioner, as well as our various agencies and the Bijzondere Bijstands Eenheid."

"Your Dutch antiterrorist force," Grant said.

Zahn nodded. "In the event they are needed. All the numbers for contact are on the folder. The Dutch police will assist you in any way you require. Two undercover officers are at the Zuider now, keeping watch, as Agent Mercier requested. They have your cell number and will establish contact when there's any activity on his part."

"Excellent," Grant said. All the agencies were on the same page and working together. COMPASS had been established to further that aim, and this cooperation underlined its success. Jurisdiction wouldn't be a problem, thank goodness.

The punctilious Zahn added, "I, of course, am merely

a messenger in this case, but if you need anything else from Interpol, please call me directly and I will coordinate."

He placed several more papers on the desk, including copies of the sketch Marie had done, snapped his case shut and turned to go. "Ms. Beauclair, my abject apologies if I offended you." He gave her another perfunctory bow, then offered his hand to Grant. "Agent Tyndal. Best of luck with your investigation. We are depending on you to curtail these abductions and resolve things quickly to everyone's relief and satisfaction."

"Thank you for your prompt assistance," Grant said, aping the man's formality.

He saw himself out. No sooner had the door closed than Marie rolled her eyes and flopped down on the nearest bed. "Insufferable prick! See what I put up with? Pat the little girl on the head and treat her like the wallpaper!"

Grant laughed. "He's a pencil pusher. And to be fair, he doesn't know you're an agent. No one knows but the Company, Mercier and me. You played your part well at the consulate." He couldn't resist teasing her a little. "And admit it, your appearance *is* deliberate. I'll bet you're not even a real blonde."

She gave him a go-to-hell look. "Like you'll ever find out."

Grant held up both hands in surrender, unable to squelch his grin.

On her feet again, she paced to the table and rifled through the papers Zahn had left. "So, we do what now? Wait and see who Onders contacts?"

"That's the plan."

He could see the exact instant she suddenly recalled

the man's location. "You knew," she said, her tone accusatory. "How did you know. And don't give me that bit about feeling it on that paper he touched."

How could he explain other than that? Grant shrugged and tried to distract her. "Lucky guess. You ready to go find something to eat? I'm starving and they have the best breakfasts in the world here."

Her blue eyes narrowed. "You're not getting off that easy, Tyndal. I want to know how you knew he went to the Zuider."

"What can I tell you? Nothing that you'll believe. I just knew, that's all. How do *you* memorize entire pages of type? Maps? Faces? I can't do that, and I don't know anyone else who can, either. How do cows know when a storm's coming?"

"Barometric pressure! Ozone in the air? How the heck should I know?" She huffed and crossed her arms. "Now you're comparing me to *cows?* God, you're worse than Zahn! I think I'd rather be ignored!"

"I was comparing *myself* to the cows. Oh, just forget it!" Exasperated, he shook his head and grabbed his jacket off the chair. "You definitely need coffee. C'mon, let's go."

"What if we run into this Onders or whatever his name is? We aren't that far from the Zuider," she warned. "He would recognize me."

Grant stopped and looked into her eyes, searching for the fear she must feel. She hid it pretty well, actually. He brushed a blond tendril off her brow and tucked it behind her ear. "I'll be there. He won't hurt you."

She stepped back out of reach and shot him a look

of disbelief. "You think I'm *scared* of him? No, you idiot! If he sees me, he'll know we're onto him and run! We'll never get him or who he's working for."

With a heavy sigh, she retrieved the bag she had brought from her apartment and pulled out the cap she had worn yesterday. "I better wear this." She twisted her hair, piled it on top of her head and put the cap on over it. Then she gave him another glare. "Maybe that will help you forego any blond jokes that come to mind."

A double espresso, maybe two, Grant was thinking. She definitely wasn't a morning person. But he'd bet blond *was* her real hair color. She was too sensitive about it for it not to be.

As if he'd ever find out.

Grant felt marginally human after they had eaten, and he had forgiven Marie for snapping at him earlier. They now knew where Onders had gone, and Grant knew his reading of the paper clue had been right.

He was talking on his phone, coordinating with the police as they walked. She was quiet, probably formulating questions for him as soon as he finished.

"Watch out!" He grabbed her arm and snatched her out of the way as a bike rider missed her by inches. "You have to be careful if you get on the red paths," he warned. "Those are for bikes, and they'll run right over you." He'd pulled her right up against him.

She pushed out of his grasp and rubbed her biceps.

"Why do you keep acting so concerned, Tyndal? It's not necessary. You think that's part of the rescue job, the protector bit?"

He nodded. "Well, yeah. But even if it wasn't, what's wrong with a little human concern?"

"A little. That's the key." She turned, gesturing with one hand for emphasis. "Say I'd been killed by Onders before you got there. There would have been an initial outcry. People would go, 'Ah, that's awful! Poor girl.' Then they'd go on to the next news story, and you'd go on to your next job without another thought. See, I get that and I understand it, so you don't have to pretend."

"What the hell are you talking about?"

She wrinkled her nose. "We all like to think we're so important, but the truth is I wouldn't be missed much, if at all, and I know it. I'm just saying you don't have to act all worried and hover like you care."

"That's ridiculous. I do care. And your family would grieve if anything bad happened to you. They'd feel guilty for the rest of their lives because they hadn't been able to afford the ransom."

She sighed. "Ah, Tyndal, you're assuming, and we both know what that says about you. I haven't seen my family in years. The only person left who's actually related by blood is my mom, and I don't even know where she lives."

"What about friends? I know you have friends."

"Sure. My coworkers. And they," she said with an emphatic pause, "didn't bother to send anyone to extract me, did they? No, a stranger came, one who didn't know me from a hole in the ground. On orders from someone who's only interest is my weird ability to memorize things."

What could he say? She was right about that. He'd

be pissed, too. And bitter. She didn't seem all that bitter, though. It was more like something she had reluctantly accepted long ago and gotten used to. "Well, I came after you and now I know you. You need a friend, you've got one."

Her smile was sweet, dimpled and patently false. "Thanks, but that's okay. I'd just as soon keep this on a professional basis. I'll have your back if you need help. That's the way the game's played, and I know my part."

"Damn!" He blew out a breath of frustration. "Somebody sure gave you a callous way of looking at life. Don't you trust anyone at all?"

Her brow furrowed as she thought about the question. Then she shook her head. "Just myself."

"You can trust me."

"Maybe I do a little, subconsciously anyway. I did sleep last night."

"Maybe there's hope for you yet," he muttered, taking her arm again and linking it with his when she edged too close to the bike path. "Humor me, would you? I don't care if you have to act."

She laughed and gave his arm a rough little squeeze. "I can't help but like you, Tyndal. You are so naive it's downright funny."

He put his free hand over hers. "Stop gloating. Just because you sneaked out on me and made me look stupid, don't think you'll get away with that again."

"Wouldn't dream of it," she promised. Her smile looked real this time, but he didn't trust it much.

He wished they hadn't had this conversation. Now it wasn't only her physical well-being he had to worry about. She'd been hurt somehow and in some way he was afraid he couldn't fix.

Sometimes the worst scars of all didn't show.

Chapter 7

Marie felt fairly comfortable with Tyndal today. He was holding her hand, and she'd almost gotten used to that. Sort of liked it, too. Maybe that wasn't wise, but she didn't want to hurt his feelings. "Where are we going?"

He pocketed the phone he was still holding. "I thought maybe we'd hit a few of the little shops, walk down to the city center. You haven't been here before, and there's no reason why you shouldn't enjoy it while we have some free time. I'm afraid the museums will be too crowded, though, and we should stay ready to respond."

"We should be watching his hotel." She hated to protest because she really did want to tour the city. Who knew when she'd get another chance?

"The commissioner assured me the police would handle it. We'll still be close by. I said we'd relieve two of the officers at nine tonight. If anything breaks, they'll call." He smiled at her and nodded at one of the quaint little shops. "Any particular kind of souvenir you'd like to buy?"

"A diamond, of course!" she said, laughing. "Isn't that what this place is famous for?"

"Well, they're pretty good at cutting them up, so I hear. Hope your credit card balance is healthy."

"Not *that* healthy," she admitted. "Let's look in there." She darted into one of the shops and began browsing, thinking a small piece of delftware would be nice.

They shopped for several hours and spent the rest of the day seeing the sights. After a late dinner, they retrieved Grant's car from the parking lot and went to work.

Marie had to remind herself why she was there. Grant had kept her so busy that the events of the past few days had faded. It was as if their little sojourn had turned into a vacation. When she mentioned it to him, he admitted that distraction had been his intent.

"You needed to regroup and unwind a bit," he had said.

Maybe he was right about that, but she hated his presuming that she couldn't handle it, that she had to be coddled. Nobody coddled her unless she instigated it to further her objectives. Nobody.

At nine o'clock that evening, Grant and Marie took their turn doing surveillance. They sat in Grant's vehicle, parked on the sidewalk, half a block from the Zuider with a clear view of the main entrance.

There were only three exits, and the other two were being manned by another duo of local police. He and

Marie were watching the front because that was the most likely one Onders would use if he left. He had no reason to believe anyone was onto him.

Stakeouts were a necessary evil, usually boring as hell and uncomfortable, too. Gallons of coffee consumed in order to stay awake presented the problem of bathroom breaks. Having a partner helped. Of course, the person you were paired with made a difference.

He and Marie had already discussed the downside of the duty, listed their pet peeves and laughed about them. She hated humming, smoking and tongue clicking. He steamed over slurping, drumming fingers on the dash and incessant throat clearing.

Conversation quickly gave out as a general rule and left little other than the annoying munch of whatever snacks were involved and the interminable sighs of discontent. Surprisingly that was not so this time.

He certainly wouldn't classify Marie as a chatterbox, and neither was he. They spoke occasionally when a topic occurred, but it didn't seem forced, and the silences were agreeable, even comfortable. Points for her.

He liked that she didn't try too hard to be charming and sound smart. She was both without any effort at all, and he wished he could tell her that without sounding as if he were coming on to her.

Her soft laugh drew his attention. "What?" he asked, smiling at her delighted expression.

"Look there." She pointed to a couple on bicycles across the street. They must be eighty if they're a day!"

The two were stealing glances at each other as they

pedaled and giggled about something one of them must have said. Grant watched them until they rode out of sight. "Statistics prove older people are happier. Did you know that? You'd think it would be the other way around, wouldn't you?"

"Oh, I don't know. I guess most of your problems are either solved or accepted by then. You needn't worry so much about impressing people anymore and can just be yourself."

Grant thought about that and what made her say it. "You worry about impressions?" He had been thinking the opposite about her only moments before.

"Only relating to the job. You know, ditzy blonde so that I'm underestimated. Party girl so I can flit around, eavesdropping."

He nodded and slid a glance over her dark jeans, black sweater and the cap that covered her hair. "Androgynous spy."

She laughed again. "Androgynous?"

"Not exactly. The bumps on the front sort of give you away." And the beautiful features, the graceful hands and that rounded little butt that filled out those Calvin Klein's to perfection, he didn't add.

"Ah, you noticed the bumps?"

"Nice bumps. Who wouldn't?"

"Well, thanks. I think."

"You're welcome. Seriously, do you run into many problems on the job? I mean, you must get a lot of unwanted attention with that butterfly thing you do. Propositions and such. Isn't your cover sort of an open invitation to hits?"

"The worst part of the job, but I'm getting pretty good at duck-and-run with a smile over the shoulder. Gets dicey sometimes," she admitted.

Grant couldn't help the stab of anger at men who would take advantage of a young woman who appeared guileless and not too brainy. "That's dangerous ground, Marie. Maybe you should rethink your approach and tone it down a little."

Her smile faded to a stony frown. "And maybe you should do a little review on your own training. Whatever weapon works best at the time, you use it."

"Mind my own business, huh?"

"Got that right." She pouted for a little while, then blew out a sigh and shifted in her seat. "Is there any more coffee in that Thermos?"

Grant handed it over and watched her drink from the cup top. She slurped noisily, intentionally, her gaze locked on his, deliberately trying to annoy him, daring him to comment. He knew she wanted a fight, so he merely smiled, clicked his tongue and said. "Lovely manners."

She finished the coffee quietly and screwed the cap back on. "Okay, truce?"

"Truce," he agreed.

It was a long shift and he'd rather spend it with her than alone or with anyone else. He liked being with her, period. She was an enigma, that was for sure. Unpredictable, fascinating and beautiful as quicksilver.

And a bigger distraction than any he had experienced on a mission. Grant locked his fingers behind his head and concentrated on the entrance to the hotel.

* * *

Marie was up early the next morning in spite of their late night on watch. She showered and dressed for another day of exploring the city. There seemed to be little else to do but kill time until they had a break in the case.

She figured if Onders didn't make a move soon, however, he'd be arrested and interrogated in hopes of discovering who had hired him.

When she returned to the bedroom, Grant was already dressed and on the phone. Suddenly, he flipped it shut. "The commissioner. We've got a situation."

Without further explanation, he started getting his things together. Marie rushed to catch up, and they were soon ready to leave.

He still hadn't told her what was going on or where they were going, but she held her questions, giving him time to formulate a plan.

At the moment he was frowning over a small tourist map.

"Is Onders on the move?" she asked finally.

"Another abduction, one of the clerks at the U.S. consulate at Museumplein. Never been there."

"Get the car," Marie told him. "If we cut through from this street on Van Baerlestraat, it's a straight shot."

He frowned a second, then his expression cleared. "Oh, the map's in your head."

"Yep. The consulate's near the Van Gogh Museum. Know where that is?"

He nodded and they hurried downstairs. "When did he take her?" Marie asked.

"Early this morning."

"On our watch?"

"Maybe, but Onders didn't come out that front door. That much I know. Maybe he didn't do it."

Marie felt a burning in the pit of her stomach. She could almost taste whatever it was that had knocked her out when she had been taken, and she remembered the feeling of outrage when she woke up.

Valet parking delivered Grant's car to the entrance and they hopped in. Grant had automatically gone to the driver's side even though she was the one who knew exactly how to get where they were going. Typical male, Marie thought with a huff, but didn't waste time arguing.

"We have to find her, Grant," she said, then recalled those questions she'd never had a chance to ask. "How'd you locate me?"

"Your locator chip. She doesn't have one."

"I know it's there, but to tell you the truth, I didn't give a thought to depending on it. So, they knew where I was all the time? The Company, I mean? Why didn't they—"

"We were detailed to do it. It's our case now."

"Well, can't you…zone in on her or whatever you claim to do? If you have something she would have touched? You did it with Onders's little list."

"Nope. Doesn't work that way. She would have to be the one deciding where to go, or at least know where she was going." He glanced over at her. "A believer now, are you?"

"Not really, just desperate to try anything and everything. Aren't you?"

"Sure I am, and we do have an agent who's an empath. He might be able to locate her if *she* knows where she is. That's a big if, though. I'll call as soon as we reach the consulate."

They were all a bunch of nuts at COMPASS, Marie thought, but she held on to the hope that she was wrong. Surely the government wouldn't put so much faith and funds into a group of self-defined psychics if they hadn't proved they could do *something* out of the ordinary.

What if it were true? Grant *was* pretty convincing. Suppose the team did consist of empaths, mind readers and vibe seekers like him? Would she fit in? Her edge wouldn't seem all that keen stacked against theirs, would it? She shook her head. Man, what a strange decision to have to make, based on criteria that was even stranger.

Chapter 8

Marie and Grant reached the consulate in under six minutes. After identifying themselves, they spoke with Acting Chief Brunson to get the details.

Marie automatically stood aside and took the subordinate role for practical reasons. Grant might obtain more information directly than she could, since they were dealing with a man.

"Cynthia Rivers was abducted from her flat on Ruysdahl between two and three this morning," he informed them. "Her roommate, who tends bar at one of the nightspots in the Center, found Cynthia missing when she came in from her late shift. She said there were signs of a struggle."

"Could we see her file?" Grant asked.

"Our personnel records are strictly confidential," Brunson said. His glance fell on a blue folder on the side of his desk.

"If you have a photo of her, that might be helpful," Grant told him. "Perhaps you could answer a few questions about her that wouldn't compromise her privacy?"

Brunson looked doubtful, but he drew the folder in front of him and opened it. A photo was clipped to the top right-hand corner, and he removed it, handing it to Grant.

Marie lasered in on the upside-down form as Grant fired off questions to distract Brunson. Then she shifted her gaze to the typed copy opposite the form and recorded that. The fifteen seconds or so that Grant afforded her had to be enough because Brunson closed the folder and set it aside.

"Thank you, sir. You've been a big help." Then Grant took her arm and turned to leave. "Let's go."

She prayed they could find the young woman before she was harmed. "We're going to her address, aren't we?" Marie asked after they'd left Brunson's office.

"Yeah. Your head map still working? Where is it?"

Marie stopped and closed her eyes, visualizing the map of the city she'd committed to memory. "It's a straight shot going toward the A10 exit."

"How efficient you are, little MapQuest," he said with a short laugh. "What would I do without you?"

"I doubt Rivers will be ransomed, Grant. She's a small-town girl, went to a community college, then on scholarship to Mercer University. Her father's a landscaper and her mom's a housewife. They live in Shelby, Arkansas."

"You got that from her file? Reading it upside down?"

"Are you impressed?" she asked with a smile.

"Utterly astounded. Let's go find this young lady."

When they reached the apartment building, police cars blocked the street. People were going in and coming out like ants.

Marie didn't envy the police collecting evidence. "Not exactly a secure scene, is it?"

Grant strong-armed his way through the crowd near the entry, flashed his badge and asked for the chief inspector. Marie held up her badge and followed in his wake, curious to see what he would do next.

He had a few words with the inspector, who acted friendly enough to a strange American agent elbowing his way into an ongoing investigation.

Grant could be pushy—that was for sure. She didn't realize just how pushy until he reached behind him and grabbed her hand, dragging her along to the apartment.

Cynthia Rivers had fought for her freedom. It hadn't been nearly as easy as when the kidnapper took her, Marie thought. "Could this have been a different guy, maybe? The timing for one thing. And there were never signs of a struggle."

Grant shrugged. "Maybe." He left her at the door and went inside the room as if he belonged there.

What the hell was he doing? Contaminating the scene, for one thing. Hindering the forensics person, for another. The gloved woman didn't look quite as agreeable as the inspector had and was railing at Grant in Dutch.

He ignored her, picking up first one scattered object,

then another and another. Eyes closed and tuning her out. Or maybe tuning in to something else.

Now he was holding a bath sponge, of all things, squeezing it between his hands. He sniffed it and made a face. Marie felt the hairs rise on the back of her neck.

Could he really get something like that? She watched as he slowly placed it back on the floor where he'd found it.

"Enough!" cried the forensics woman.

"Yes, that's enough," Grant agreed. He nodded to the irate examiner as he stood. "Thank you, and I apologize for the interruption."

He went over to the window, took out his cell phone and made a call. Marie stayed where she was by the doorway until he joined her.

"I can't believe they let you do that," Marie exclaimed.

"I told the inspector I was looking for similarities to the last victim of the Embassy Kidnapper. He had orders to cooperate."

"What *were* you doing with that bath sponge, by the way?"

Instead of answering, he took her hand to lead her back outside. "We're going to Gouda."

She started to jerk her hand away out of habit, but didn't. It felt somehow right to let him hold it at the moment. She even threaded her fingers through his. "Gouda? Where they make that cheese?"

"That's where he was headed with her."

"Onders?"

Grant inclined his head and shrugged. "Like you said, the M.O. is different. He overpowered her, probably knocked her out. There was chloroform on the sponge—pretty much dissipated now, though. Maybe it evaporated too quickly to be effective."

"That forensics lady was about to knock *you* out!"

"I don't blame her. But I had to pick up on the kidnapper's energy."

"And you did?"

Grant nodded. "He carried her over his shoulder. He was thinking about where he could stash her and worrying about the lack of planning. This was a rush job, maybe to make up for losing you."

"So how'd you get Gouda out of all that?"

"He was going there with her. Had to. That means there's probably someone there calling the shots."

Marie hated to leave without seeing more of Amsterdam, but finding this woman was the top priority. Catching the kidnapper ran a close second. She was as eager as Grant was to take up the chase.

When had she begun to trust his instincts or whatever it was that led him? Marie wondered. Looking back, it was probably when they found that Onders was actually in Amsterdam.

"What about Onders? Is he still under surveillance?"

"I hope so. Call and inform them we won't be relieving them today, would you?" He reached in his pocket and handed her his phone and a card with the number. "This is the force coordinator. Don't mention the lead we're following just yet. I could be wrong."

"You? Wrong?" She laughed as she punched in the number. "Oh, right, that 20 percent margin of error we have to worry about."

"I'm pretty sure about it," Grant said, obviously not taking offense. He even seemed amused by her doubt.

Minutes later she related the news to Grant. "Onders is in the wind, and they just discovered it. He must have sneaked out of his hotel somehow and grabbed the clerk."

"It seemed like a different energy. Not the same thought patterns."

"You want to explain that?" she asked, trying to sound polite when she wanted to shake him till his teeth rattled.

"Later. I'm thinking right now."

Fortunately for him, Grant didn't sound petulant or annoyed, only distracted, so she let it go.

The ride to Gouda proved uneventful and silent. Marie wondered if he thought talking about his findings would jinx the op.

She gave him his time to think and enjoyed the scenery. The day was great, sunny and cool and perfect for open windows to enjoy the sweetness of the air. Small wonder it smelled sweet, since this was the flower capital of the world. Acres of them somewhere nearby she imagined as she inhaled.

It seemed so unreal that they were out chasing evil on a day like today. Even more so when they arrived in the picturesque little town of Gouda.

"What a fairy-tale place! Look at that spire. Wow, that has to be a thousand years old! And they have an open-air market. Turn—you can't drive through there. Pedestrians only."

"I know. I've been here before, but it's been a long time. My dad was stationed in Germany, and Holland was one of our favorite vacation spots."

"You mentioned before that you were a military brat. That must have been interesting." She had another piece of the Grant Tyndal puzzle. He hadn't shared much about himself at all since they'd met, and she was curious. "It's not fair that you know almost everything about me from my file and I know hardly anything about you."

"Not much to know," he replied, "and none of it secret except what I do for a living. You already know that."

None of it secret, huh? Well, that was one thing they didn't have in common, and she wasn't inclined to share any of her own Kodak moments. The personal Q&A should end right here. He might have the facts in her file but nothing she hadn't been willing to reveal.

"So what do we do now?" she asked.

"Find a place to stay, I guess, since there's nothing else we can do for the moment. We'll have to wait for the commissioner to return my call. He promised to get an address here for a phone number."

Marie resented his keeping things from her. "What phone number?"

He sighed, pulled up on the sidewalk in front of a three-story building and parked. "He was thinking of a number he had to call. So far, that's all I know. With any luck Onders is headed here, too, if he isn't the one who took her."

"They're with the Hofstad Group, you think?"

"Maybe, maybe not. This…well, it feels like its motivated more by greed than a zealous political or religious act. At least where this perpetrator is concerned."

"Vibes again, huh?" she asked, realizing only after the words were out that she sounded condescending.

He shot her a look of exasperation. "Look, I get that you think I'm making this up as we go, but spare me the sarcasm, will you?"

"Sorry," she said, ducking her head a little and wincing. "It's just strange, that's all. You have been on the money so far—I'll give you that much. Maybe if you explained it more, if it can be explained, it wouldn't seem quite so hocus-pocus."

He looked her straight in the eye. "I touch objects and through residual energy I collect their history, initially their most immediate history."

"For instance?"

He thought for a minute, his hands still resting on the steering wheel. "Say I'm holding a very old clay pot. The energy would have, like, layers. First, I'd get the person who evaluated its age, then the archaeologist who discovered it, the ancient who used it and finally the one who created it. I'd get what they felt at the moment, general emotions or impressions. Now and then, words, if they thought in words. People don't always. And sometimes they think in a language I don't understand."

"What about the people who owned it in between?" she asked.

He shook his head. "Only if they spent a lot of energy on it or a lot of time handling it. I have to concentrate, then stop at the level that reveals what I need. It's taken years of experimenting and training to control it. Well, *usually* I control it. As I told you, my success rate is only around 80 percent."

"So, that sponge you found. The kidnapper had it last and invested a little time doctoring it up."

"Then tossed it as useless," Grant said. "It belonged to Cynthia. He found it in her bathroom. That's where he waited for her."

She still didn't believe it, but she believed he believed. "What about touching people? They'd have a purer energy, right? Why can't you read minds?"

He smiled and placed a palm on the side of her face. "Right now you're humoring me. You think I'm a pretty good guesser. The list we found was in Dutch, so Amsterdam was a fair bet. You can't explain Gouda, but they make great cheese here so you decided to come along for the ride."

Marie brushed his hand away and scoffed. "I wasn't thinking that at all."

He laughed. "Sure you were, but no, I'm not telepathic. It's just written all over your pretty face."

Pretty? Without any makeup, wearing her worst color, hair hidden under a baseball cap? He thought she was pretty. She felt herself blush. "Now who's being sarcastic?" she demanded with a grin.

"False modesty doesn't become you a bit, Beauclair. You know how beautiful you are. You work on and use it, too. You already admitted that."

"I'm not working on it now. And I'm not telling you anything else."

He tapped a finger on her nose. "I'll bet when you applied to the Company, you played it down then, too. No war paint, hair pulled straight back, maybe even darkened a few shades. Wore a gray suit not designed to flatter, pants to cover up those fantastic legs." He paused, squinting at her face. "And glasses, I'm thinking. Yeah. You'd have worn those, ugly horn-rims. Close?"

She simply stared at him. How could he possibly know that? "You're guessing, that's all. Any idiot would know I wouldn't apply for a *job* looking like a brainless twit, even if I was going to use it as a cover later."

He laughed. "Come on, mouse, let's go register. Want to share quarters again? You know it will be more convenient if we do."

She opened her own door and hopped out, not waiting for him to play the gent. "Well, I'm not sure about that, Tyndal. Knowing you think I'm *pretty* might just make me nervous."

He grabbed their bags out of the trunk, tossed her hers and grinned. "Even if I promise not to touch your...things?"

Lord, she hadn't had time to consider that. What if he really *could* get feelings, emotions and even words?

She grasped her little tote closer to her body, then shook her head at the weird thought.

But he had known about the gray suit and glasses. A good guess, indeed.

Chapter 9

Marie didn't bother offering any more objections. She didn't really want to stay alone, especially not after hearing about the latest kidnapping. Only one chance in a million it would happen again to her, but just having Grant around had seemed to give her a feeling secure enough to let her sleep. She still could hardly believe that.

"You must be trying for some kind of brownie points with whoever foots your expense account," she said.

"The taxpayers, honey, of which you are one, hopefully, now that you have a steady career. So you can thank me for saving you money." He held open the door to the ancient building and stood aside for her to enter.

"Thanks...*honey*," she replied as she brushed past him.

She was beginning to like him more and more. Even if he was a little off the wall. Okay, a *lot*.

He hadn't hit on her, and she trusted his word that he wouldn't. Trust was a fine commodity she found extremely hard to come by.

She actually had gone to sleep in the same room with him and had slept better than she usually did. Maybe that was due to exhaustion from the kidnapping ordeal and all that followed, but she didn't think so.

Tonight she would find out, and that was another reason she didn't protest sharing a room with him again. She needed to know if that purely instinctual episode of trust was an aberration or if she had actually unloaded some of her past baggage.

They approached the desk and were greeted by a tall, handsome fellow with an ingratiating smile. He introduced himself as Pieter Selton. Grant presented their passports and offered his official credit card.

"You are with the American government, I see. Welcome to Gouda. If I may be of assistance to you, please do not hesitate to ask."

Grant thanked him and refused the offer of help with their bags, since they had only the two.

There was no elevator, and the stairs to their room were very steep and narrow, as they were in most old buildings. He insisted on her preceding him up the stairs, and she felt a little self-conscious, knowing his face was only inches from her behind.

Was he checking out her buns? She tried not to twitch as she climbed. No point in teasing him. It wouldn't gain her anything. Still, she wondered what he would do if she weren't so careful not to do anything provocative. Would he cave on his promise and make a pass?

Well, he might. And wasn't that what she feared the most?

Not necessarily, a little voice inside her head answered. In fact, what she would normally term fear felt more like anticipation. This was not good.

He placed his free hand on her waist as they reached the top of the stairs. "To the right," he said.

The urge to jerk away from his touch just didn't occur, she noted. How strange was that? Of course, she had learned to repress that urge when she knew it would make her seem standoffish.

Men touched her fairly often, and she allowed it if they were merely being polite. Handshakes were almost mandatory in her business, and she could even manage the occasional hug without an openly negative response. But with Grant she no longer felt that automatic wariness.

She could appear sexy and approachable and sometimes used that in her line of work. Okay, often used it. But she never followed through. All in all, she figured she did pretty well in disguising how she really was.

Grant was smiling at her when she looked at him. Had he guessed she was mostly show? Was that why he had assured her that their temporary partnership would stay platonic?

He unlocked the door to their room and went in first to check it out. "Hey, this is quaint, don't you think?"

"Nice," she agreed, dropping her bag onto one of the single beds. They were antiques, as were the dresser, desk and chairs. "No television, I see. This place is *really* old world!"

"No bath in the room, either. It's down the hall." He walked over to the window. "Nice view, though. See?"

Marie joined him at the window. "Is this some kind of trip down memory lane for you? I get the feeling you've been here before."

"As a kid. It hasn't changed much. New linens maybe, but the rest looks the same. My parents and I were here about twenty years ago. Had a great time."

He looked down at her, still smiling. "Don't you like to revisit old times?"

Marie tore her gaze from his and looked out the window again. "Not especially." Not at all, under any circumstances.

"Ah. Well, I guess I was spoiled by my folks. They always found the neatest things to see and do when we were on vacation. Probably because we had so little time together, the three of us. It was always quality. Still is."

"You're an only child?" she asked, curious about his nostalgia. She had none of that, for sure.

"Oh, yeah, and I loved every second of it," he admitted. "With the possible exception of when my dad was away and I was responsible for looking after my mother. That's a heavy detail for a kid, and I always worried I wouldn't live up."

"But I'll bet you did," she guessed and sighed, feeling a longing she couldn't explain. "You're close, you and your parents."

"Except for minor upheavals. Dad had a fit when I joined the navy instead of the army, but he got over it. Mom wasn't crazy about my wife—said we didn't suit. Turns out she was right and I should have listened."

Marie backed away from him. "You're married?"

"Not anymore. Long time ago. It lasted about a year, and enough said about that," he declared. "We all make mistakes and learn from 'em."

Marie didn't push, even though her curiosity was killing her. What had happened? Had his mother come between him and his wife? None of her business.

She did appreciate how open he was, though. Not a speck of hesitation in answering her questions, and he even volunteered information. Every agent she had known so far had been a closed book and she hadn't cared. This one intrigued her. He was actually very friendly. She sort of envied his outgoing nature, wishing she could be more like that.

"I never took the plunge myself," she offered, testing the newness of real congeniality. "I was engaged once, but it didn't work out."

"Better to know up front, that's for sure. What about your parents? You said you didn't know where your mother lived. I read in your file that both your parents live in Atlanta."

They had. Maybe they still did. Marie had no clue where they were now. She wished she did so she could avoid the place at all costs. Grant was waiting for a reply, but she didn't give it.

She turned away from him and the window. "Shouldn't the police have called with that address by now?"

"Ah, subject change. You don't like to talk about

your family. Got it. And you're right, I do need to follow up on that and check in with control."

He hesitated, then asked, "Should I tell Mercier that you're at least interested in the job with COMPASS?"

Busy testing the comfort of the bed by bouncing on the edge of it, she stopped. "I don't know. Would you and I be partnered?"

"I've always worked cases alone," he said. Arms crossed, he leaned against the window frame. "Until this one."

She flapped a hand in his direction. "Sorry to intrude on your mission, but I'm here and I'm staying until we're through, so get over it."

"Oh, I'm pretty much over it," he told her with a grin. He fished his cell phone out of his pocket to make his calls. "I'm even getting used to the distraction and taking orders from you. They might have to retrain me to work on my own when I get back."

Marie scoffed, secretly pleased at his teasing. She left him talking on the phone and went down the hall to the bathroom. She needed some space and wanted to be away from him to think.

Was she getting too involved with this guy? Shouldn't she be throwing up barriers or something? Maybe she ought to put Grant the man right out of her mind and see him only as Grant the agent, the means to an end.

How was she supposed to do that when he was being so friendly, talking so frankly to her about his personal relationships and looking at her with such guileless appreciation. And all the while keeping his distance as he promised. She had never met anyone quite like Grant Tyndal.

When she returned to the room, Grant was tucking away his phone. "The consulate has received a ransom call already. Couldn't be traced, of course. The demand's the same but the fuse is shorter and they won't be stalled. We have until tomorrow night to find her."

"What about the number you psyched up?" she asked.

"Got a name and address for it. It's a landline, located on Prouter. Belongs to a Dr. Harold Shute. Interpol's got nothing on him. We'll need a map to find his place." He put the laptop case on the bed and unzipped it. "Your turn to work."

She went online and quickly found a map. "Prouter's not listed." Five more searches gave different maps of the city and surrounding suburbs. "It's just not on the maps, Grant. Not as a road, street or lane. Must be way out of town." She did a search on Dr. Harold Shute and found an obituary. "He's dead. Died years ago."

"Dead? And still paying his phone bill? Something's screwy. I'll go down and ask around," he said, and started for the door.

"I'm coming, too. Wouldn't want you to get lost."

This time she went down the stairs behind him, barely resisting the urge to reach out and touch his hair. Was it soft or bristly? she wondered. What would he do if he felt her hand on his head? Marie expelled a harsh breath, angry at her thoughts.

At the bottom of the stairs, he reached out and took her hand. Didn't even stop to think about it, she noticed.

He just took it in his as if he had every right. And she didn't resist.

He approached the desk clerk and asked for directions to Prouter. The desk clerk's brow wrinkled as he thought about it. "Sorry, I don't know of it," he admitted.

"Have you ever heard of a Dr. Shute in this area?"

"No."

Grant thanked him and continued on outside. "Somebody has to know where Prouter is," he muttered.

They canvassed several shops and asked people on the street but got only puzzled looks and apologies. "The post office," Marie suggested, spying it up ahead.

There, they had better luck. Harold Shute was on record, but Prouter was not an address on their books. "Then how would this Shute get his phone bills?" Grant demanded. "They have to send them somewhere."

"He has a postal box," the clerk replied. She checked it and there were two bills in it, one posted two weeks earlier. "The street or road name is probably an old one and has been changed to another," she said. "Perhaps you should try city hall. They should have records of the property."

Even there and at the public library, no one could find the elusive name Prouter.

"A typo," Marie guessed finally. "It has to be a bad listing."

"Let's go back to the hotel, get on the computer and search all the possibilities, then."

They worked on it the rest of the afternoon.

"I'm wiped out," Grant said, his frustration apparent

as he stretched out across his bed. "Where the hell *is* the place?"

"Take a break and call for room service," Marie suggested, typing in yet another variation of the word.

He rang the desk and ordered. They ate in silence, each lost in thoughts of what could be happening to Cynthia the consulate clerk while they scrambled around trying to find her.

"She's not going to die," Marie declared. "We'll find her."

"I wish I knew how," Grant said, wiping a hand over his face, then letting it rest on his chest. "This is maddening!"

Marie reached over and laid a hand on his shoulder. "C'mon, Grant. You're acting as if this is your fault. Look how much you've done already, and we won't stop now. But you need to regroup a little. We both do."

He placed a hand over hers and gave it a squeeze. "I like you, you know that? I like how you stay so positive when it looks as if we're at a dead end here."

"We are no such thing," she assured him. "Something will pop, you'll see." Marie leaned over and kissed him. The act surprised her almost as much as it did him.

She felt his lips tense, then relax and welcome hers. Passion flared, but he banked it quickly.

He looked up at her as she broke the kiss. "Please tell me you're releasing me from that stupid promise I made to you."

Chapter 10

Marie held his gaze. Then she closed her eyes and kissed him again. He'd find out soon enough she wasn't all she was advertising, but she did want this kiss and she wanted it badly. Whatever happened next would just have to happen.

Any moment now she'd pull back, put him in his place, show him she wasn't going to be his lay of the day. But the kiss went on.

His hands caressed her face, her neck, her shoulders and finally, when she thought she might have to plead, her breasts. He didn't hurry, and she wished he would. The sooner he reached a point that brought her to her senses, the better.

But that point seemed really elusive right now, she

thought, as she reveled in the way his hands felt on her, sliding beneath her shirt, down the back of her jeans. That groan was meant as a protest, she thought as it emerged, but it sounded like encouragement, even to her. Oh, well, why not?

He slid her shirt over her head, unsnapped her bra and discarded it. Marie simply closed her eyes and abandoned herself to the feelings, to the mounting need he roused with his hands and mouth.

She felt him pull her body against his, loving the way they fit together so perfectly if only these clothes weren't in the way.

"You know where this is going," he muttered, interspersing his words with hot kisses that were landing everywhere.

"I know," she gasped. "Please don't be disappointed."

He laughed, a growling sound that reverberated through her like a shock wave of pleasure. Sure he found it funny now, but soon…

He lifted her slightly and unsnapped her jeans. She wriggled them off while he stripped. "Oh, my," she whispered, her gaze trapped by the sight of him.

"Flattery will get you anywhere," he whispered against her neck.

She melted on top of him, moving every way she could to draw him deeper still. A wildness suffused her, something she had never experienced in all her life. The urge to give and give, to please, to grasp pleasure for herself. Such a selfless, selfish, all-encompassing rushing that went on and on with every thrust, every move.

She had never really believed in this kind of pleasure

and drew a fleeting comparison to her other experience. Sublime versus mechanical, fulfilling rather than disappointing, sustained wonder instead of heaving abruptness that showed no regard for her. Grant kissed, he touched, he made love as if his one mission in life was to share everything he was. How could she not embrace it, embrace the one who seemed to give without any reservation?

Retreating into herself never even occurred this time. Full and eager participation was the only option. She writhed against him, bowed beneath him and reveled in how her mind numbed even as the sensations claimed her fully. A glorious, wonderful bursting feeling that stole her every thought and breath.

The sound he made in his throat triggered more. Aftershocks rippled through her as his palms slid over her back and waist, coming to rest on her hips. His ragged breathing tickled her neck.

"Damn," he whispered, grazing his lips over her shoulder. "I knew it."

Marie felt his words like a splash of icy water. She pushed up and glared down at his slumberous expression. "Guess I should've told you. I'm not good at this."

His brow wrinkled in question. "What?"

She closed her eyes, not wanting to see his frown. "Not much experience. All of it disappointing."

"Disappointing to *you?*" He brushed a tendril of hair off her face with his finger.

"To all parties concerned," she admitted. Now he'd leave her alone. "Even the guy who always bragged that the worst he ever had was wonderful changed his mind."

"Was it that fiancé of yours?"

Marie hesitated a second, then nodded.

"The fool oughta be shot. You *know* he was lying, right?"

She shrugged one shoulder. "He accused me of false advertising."

"What?" Grant scoffed, shaking his head in disbelief.

Marie made a face. "He said I looked very sexy, talked that way, too, but I was obviously created by some surgeon and he might as well have bought a plastic doll."

Grant laughed. "Ah, honey, let me translate that for you. He beat you across the finish line, and you didn't complete the race. His fault, of course, and he was afraid you'd complain. Maybe even tell somebody about it. He figured attack was the best defense."

"So you think it was manspeak, huh?"

"At its worst. I apologize for my gender. We can be real jerks."

"You're not." Marie could have kissed him but knew that would only compound her error. "I didn't really think he suffered all that much, but neither did I feel it was worth arguing about. Better off without him."

"That was your only time?"

"That's none of your business! Have I asked you about your love life?"

"No, but I wouldn't care if you did. Other than my wife, I was never really involved with anyone for long. Even with her it wasn't…well, like this. That's what I meant when I said *I knew it.* All along I had a feeling that with you it would be different…serious."

"*Serious*? No, Grant. This was sex, plain and simple! That's all it was." She refused to meet his eyes. "You're crazy, aren't you?"

"Depends on who you ask."

"Well, I think you are," she declared, crossing her arms over her chest.

"Maybe so, but I'm telling you the truth. I like you, Marie, maybe even love you. And I think you're sexy as hell."

"I am not!"

"Sorry, my call. But I don't think sexy is determined by a woman's looks, shape or anything else that she's born with or could be manufactured by a scalpel. That goes for a man, too." He tapped her forehead. "It's what's in here…" Then he placed his hand over her heart. "And in here. It's what you feel and what you need to give and want to take."

Marie didn't know what to say, how to handle this. She'd never in her life had a conversation to equal it or anything to compare it with.

A knock at the door jerked them back to the real world. Marie was thankful for the interruption. She had no clue what Grant was talking about and didn't want to know. At least not until she'd had time to think about what had just happened.

She scrambled off him and snatched up her jeans. "Get *dressed!*" she snapped when he just lay there watching her.

Someone knocked again and he moved, obviously in no great hurry about it. She pulled on her shirt and went to the door, glancing over her shoulder to see if Grant was decent. "Who is it?"

"Pieter. I have information you wanted."

She opened the door, and the desk clerk handed her a rough drawing on a sheet of hotel stationery. "Here is a direction of sorts. I spoke with my grandfather. He once knew a Dr. Shute who lived in an old, rather isolated clinic called Alt Brouten Haus. It lies off the main road to Oudewater. However, he said the doctor has been dead for several years."

Marie took the paper and shot a triumphant look at Grant, then turned back to the desk clerk. "This is wonderfully helpful, Pieter. Thank you *very* much! And thank your grandfather for us, too."

"We are glad to be of assistance." He did look pleased. He also looked knowing as his gaze traveled the length of her and back again.

She didn't see how he could possibly guess what they'd been doing, but he seemed to do just that. Ridiculous thought.

"You are most welcome, Miss Beauclair," he said, his tone amused. "And if you two need anything else, anything at all, please let me know."

She closed the door and dashed over to Grant, offering him a high five. He complied, but he still hadn't lost that thoughtful look he'd worn before Pieter knocked.

"It was a misprint. And a house, not a street or road? *Brouten,* not *Prouter!*" she exclaimed, hoping to excite him about something other than their all-too-recent tryst.

She did *not* want to talk about that anymore. Not yet anyway. Maybe not ever because she had no idea what to say. "I *told* you something would break!"

"So you did. Maybe you're psychic and just don't know it."

"Ha! Get your shoes on and let's go investigate."

He nodded, a small smile playing around his lips, as if he were privy to something she didn't know.

"Okay, I will," he agreed, "but you might want to put your shirt on right side out before we leave."

Paris was usually beautiful in the spring, but rain grayed the day. Mamud Bahktar tried to shake off the malaise.

He turned away from the corner window of his office as his extra cell phone buzzed. He had specified no contact until the job was done. Hopefully, this was it. He flipped the phone open, put it to his ear and waited.

"We have one. I am sending her photo."

Mamud noted there was no mention of background information. "From where?" Mamud demanded, uneasiness creeping up his spine.

"Amsterdam."

"Fool!" Mamud growled. "It is too close to your base of operations."

"I had no choice in the matter. My…associate…saw the opportunity and took it."

"You did the background, I hope. Two misses are all I will allow." All he could afford, really.

A moment of silence ensued as static crackled over the phone. "Of course. Four days at most and I will have what you require."

"Or else. You will have to relocate after this. Meet me here on Friday next. Dispose of the local hires before you leave. You know what is at stake, so do not fail this time." Mamud rang off and shoved the cell phone into his pocket.

He hated dealing with incompetents, but there had been no mark more suited for this with regard to location and the opportunity to hire. The leverage over this man was perfect, and there would be no ties leading to himself, not even a money trail. He would transfer the accumulated ransoms from the numbered account Shapur had set up, and the funds would go directly to the buyer.

His record was clear, his import/export business thriving and his nefarious contacts in his own country secure. All of that would remain as it was so long as he financed the shipments of arms as he had been ordered to do. If he failed, there would be consequences. He had been warned.

Use and be used—it was the way of the world—but he used his wits. The plan was his and he was arranging the execution of it, true. But he would never actually touch the money, only collect and communicate the number of the account to the proper person. That person, another like himself who valued his place in the world, was to collect and make the buy. His part would be done. Next Friday for certain.

This mission would be complete and the arms deal could commence. The secondary objective, Mamud's own brilliant plan for a desired side effect, had already been met. He imagined now that Americans serving abroad were terrified, especially the women. None of those felt safe to remain. The operation of the enemy's embassies and consulates surely had been thrown into chaos by that fear. Perhaps that benefit would prove temporary and never be publicized, but any blow to the United States was a tribute to his own country even if he was never lauded for it.

Mamud decided he would use Shapur once more before he got rid of him. It wouldn't hurt to make an extra strike to feather his own nest with an extra ransom. Who would know or care?

Mamud would need the additional funds when his future wife was given leave to come to Paris. She was a sweet young plum with excellent connections that should provide a great return on her dowry. He patted his pocket, which held the photo of the carefully guarded morsel that would become the mother of his children.

There was another photo there—of the woman who had escaped Shapur's net. Thus far there had been no headlines, as there had been with the others.

The silence surrounding the abduction worried him.

He tried to dismiss his troubling thoughts. When he met with Shapur and received the number of the account, perhaps he should dispose of him immediately and forego any further activity. After all, the doctor was the only one who could link Mamud to this.

Mamud put the pictures of the women away and sat back in his executive chair to consider all the aspects of his plan and make a final decision.

Chapter 11

Grant followed Marie down to the car and listened to her excited directions as she guided him through the outskirts of Gouda to the road that led east.

He had to shift his focus to the case, but he had trouble doing it. So Marie wasn't ready to acknowledge what had happened between them, much less discuss it. He could wait. Unless she came down with a galloping case of total amnesia, he knew she wouldn't forget it.

It wasn't ego that made him know that. In fact, he felt pretty humbled by the whole experience. He could understand her shock. They'd known each other for less than forty-eight hours. Apparently that was all it took in his case. He'd like to believe it was only the power of suggestion, triggered by recalling his dad's similar experience when he'd met Grant's mother, but he knew better. Marie was the one.

Now she was his, at least in his own mind and heart, and he now had the forever responsibility of keeping her safe and protected. She wouldn't abide by an order that she sit this one out, though. He had a bad feeling about her coming along, but he'd just have to stay between her and danger and hope for the best.

"So, old Dr. Shute is dead and someone's still picking up his mail in town. A relative, maybe? Or has someone taken over his identity?" Marie asked. "This could be headquarters for the Hoofstads, or a satellite group."

"I guess we'll find out," Grant surmised. "It would be a perfect setup, but we can't jump to any conclusions. It's a fairly safe assumption that the mail was once delivered out there. Then someone changed that by renting a box in town and using Shute's name. Could be a relative. We need more information about the clinic and what its purpose was. An interview with Pieter's grandfather would be helpful. We probably should have done that before checking out the place."

"There's the time factor," Marie reminded him. "Cynthia Rivers could be killed while we run around asking questions. What if she's being held there? As soon as the kidnappers realize there'll be no ransom for her, she's had it."

Grant couldn't argue that. "How do we find the turn-off?"

"It's the fourth road to the left. I'm counting. How

do you think the old grandfather knew about the place? The directions are roughly drawn but pretty explicit for all that. I wonder what sort of clinic it was."

"Could be anything. Tuberculosis was rampant before and after World War II, so it could be a sanatorium. Or mental-health facility. Home for unwed mothers. Too far out of town to be a regular doctor's practice. Doesn't really matter what it was, only what it is now and who's living there."

"How do we go in?" She was too antsy, almost bouncing in her seat. Her eagerness to get that clerk to safety could jeopardize everything if she didn't calm down.

"We don't go in," Grant told her. "We're scoping it out, that's all. Tonight's better for the intrusion. I'll bring in some backup if we suspect anything fishy." He gave her a warning look. "You'll stay in the car, keep your head down and let me see if anyone's there."

"I will not!"

"And what if Onders comes to the door?"

"Oh."

"Think, Marie," he insisted. "You're too close to this to stay objective. Let me handle this."

"All right," she agreed, settling back in her seat and studying the map. "At least initially."

Grant drove down the driveway to the front of the old place. It was a gray, two-story stone building, with lots of windows on the first floor. It appeared deserted. There could be vehicles hidden from view in the three small outbuildings.

He parked in the circular driveway that fronted the

house, stopping well past the entrance. Marie rolled down her window and remained low in the seat.

"Go ahead. If anyone answers the door, you can ask directions or something. I'll stay down," Marie promised.

He pounded on the door several times and was about to give it up when he heard scuffling footsteps inside.

A short, thin, gray-haired man opened the door. Dressed in a ratty robe and slippers, he peered silently up at Grant over wire-rimmed glasses. The eyes were dark, almost black, the complexion sallow.

"I wonder if you could help me, sir," Grant said in English. "Is there a petrol station nearby?"

"Six kilometers that direction on the main road," the old fellow said, pointing. "You are American?"

"Canadian, on holiday. Grant Tyndal from Toronto. And who may I thank, sir?" Grant asked, smiling broadly. He detected an accent. British, he thought, but not precisely that.

"Dr. Shapur," the man informed him.

Grant offered his hand and met reluctant acceptance. "What a grand old house you have here, doctor. I have always been interested in architecture. Is it prewar by any chance?"

"Yes." The word was clipped, impatient. Perhaps he was frightened. Or a little off the mark mentally. Hard to tell.

"I had best be on my way, then. You've been a great help to me, Dr. Shapur. I do appreciate your time."

"Of course. Drive with care."

Grant said a cheery goodbye, returned to the car and drove back to the main road.

"Well, he isn't Shute," he told Marie.

"Not dead. He looks old, though. Maybe a former partner?"

"You were supposed to stay down and out of sight."

"I did. He didn't see me, but I saw him clearly. Perfect little vignette in the side mirror."

"Maybe he's been masquerading as Shute so he wouldn't have to move out. What do you think?"

"That I've seen his face before," Marie said, resuming a more comfortable posture and adjusting her seat belt now that they were out of sight of the house.

"You're kidding! Lately?"

"No and not in person. In an old *National Geographic* from the seventies. Research for an international studies course I took." She met Grant's questioning glance. "He's Iranian. Affiliated with the last shah of Iran. At least he was photographed with him thirty-odd years ago."

"Amazing." Grant shook his head. "How do you keep all that in your brain? You're sure?"

"Certain. I don't know his name, but his face is distinctive and hasn't changed radically. He looked old, even then. I never forget a face. Let's go back to the library."

"He said his name's Dr. Shapur. Is that familiar?"

"No. The people in the photo weren't identified, except for the shah and the royal family."

"If you can make a sketch, I'll send it in. We'll get confirmation on the name and whatever info's on record about him, hopefully by tonight."

"So, we're going back after dark. Good plan."

"*I'm* going. Alone."

"What about backup?" Marie asked.

"If the Rivers woman is being held there, I stand a better chance of getting her out if I'm by myself. Besides, the doctor might have had company in there that we didn't see. I thought he looked a little scared."

"All the more reason for you to have a partner to back you up. I'm going."

"If Onders sees you, he'll kill you, Marie. He'll know you saw him, know that's how you found him and eliminate you."

"Not if I see him first." She held up a hand to stop his protest. "Promise not to kill him unless it's unavoidable."

"Yeah, right. Have you ever killed anybody? You know what the fallout's like?"

She thought about it. "No, I haven't and I don't really want to." He wasn't buying it. "Seriously, Grant. That's not what I want."

"No, you don't, believe me. So let's just keep the temptation off the table, okay?"

Once they returned to the hotel, Grant watched as Marie took up her sketchbook and began creating a likeness. Her fingers flew, stopping only occasionally to smudge a line or prop the pad against the headboard of the bed and sit back from it to gain new perspective.

What a talent she had. Magic in her hands. He pushed back the memories she had made with those hands earlier in the day. Man, she was driving him crazy.

He wondered what she had thought of their lovemaking, but he had so far resisted the urge to tune in. All he had to do was pick up something of hers that she'd touched immediately afterward.

The hairbrush. She would have been thinking of what happened between them while she raked it through her tousled hair, wouldn't she? Or maybe that shoulder bag she'd clutched while he was driving.

But what if she hadn't thought of him at all? It was very possible she'd had her mind on where they were going, trying to rescue Cynthia Rivers. Or maybe killing Onders if they found him there. Damn, he wanted to know.

Sidling around the room, killing time while she drew, he stopped at the chair where her purse lay. Using that seemed like cheating. Or an invasion of her thoughts.

How would he like it if she were capable and did the same thing to him? With an explosive sigh, he turned away from the temptation and walked over to look out the window.

Using his ability on the job was one thing, but it seemed more like abusing it when it involved a personal matter.

"What's wrong with you?" she asked, sounding a trifle distracted by what she was doing.

"Dying of curiosity," he admitted. "Did it mean anything?"

"What?" she asked, still focused on her work.

"Us. You're acting as if nothing happened. Regretting it?"

She smiled and smudged some more. "Nope."

"Just for the record, I wasn't disappointed, not by a long shot."

"Thanks."

Grant wanted to shake her silly. "Well? Is that *all* you have to say?"

She put the sketchbook down and looked at him, her head cocked to one side. "If it's an ego boost you're looking for, then I admit the sex was great. Best ever, but let it go at that, Grant. Don't get possessive."

"That's what you're afraid of? Well, I guess that's understandable, especially after what happened to you."

She picked up the sketch again and stared down at it. "Wow, you really are psychic." Then she dropped the sarcasm and faced him again. "You have no idea what it's like, and I can't explain it. It's a control thing. I have to be in control."

He felt a little bit angry and a lot defensive. "Hey, you were the one calling the shots."

She nodded. "I know. That's why it…worked so well for us."

"Someone in your past had total control and you didn't like it. Were you forced?"

Her gaze dropped and she began working again. It was several minutes before she answered. "No, but it was close."

"Tell me," Grant suggested softly. "Sometimes it helps to talk about it, and I'll bet you never have."

Her smile was sad. "I see how you look at me, Grant. You've only seen me the way I wanted you to. The real me is someone you wouldn't even want to know. I'm not talking about the surface now."

"Tell me about you and see what happens. I'm a little deeper than you seem to think."

"Fine." She made a few more marks, then held up the drawing and examined it. "I was almost thirteen," she said. "My stepfather had been sneaking into my room for nearly a year. Just touching, talking suggestively, making me really uncomfortable."

"Surely you told somebody!"

"Of course, I'm not stupid. I told my mother, but she accused me of being jealous of her and lying just to get rid of him."

"Was she nuts?" Grant could hardly control his anger at the woman. What kind of mother would say such a thing to a child in danger?

She shrugged. "Maybe she was crazy. I got sick of it all and decided to confront him."

Grant couldn't imagine what she must have gone through with no one to turn to, no one to help her. "I hope you had a weapon."

Her chuckle was grim. "The best. Brains. He wasn't all that smart. I called him at work, had him meet me at the food court at the mall. Safety in numbers, I figured. When he got there, I told him I was going to the police if he didn't get out of town that afternoon. He freaked. Quietly, of course, and he threatened to kill my mom if I told."

"What did you do?" Grant demanded, horrified. "I hope you went to the police anyway!"

"No, I knew it would have been my word against his, and if my own mother didn't believe me, why should they?" She still focused on her work as she spoke. "But TV cop shows are really helpful. I told him about the evidence I'd collected. Semen on my sheets and under-wear. It had never gone that far, so he knew he hadn't put it there, of course."

"But you had?"

"Not really, but I told him that I had, from used

condoms I'd found in the trash in their bedroom. I told him I had a boyfriend at school, that the cops would surely wonder how a poor little girl had lost her virginity at twelve and they'd blame him for it. That was a lie, of course. I was still intact, but I must have been pretty damn convincing."

"How could you have known about sex at twelve?" Grant couldn't imagine that.

"Oh, man, you are naive, aren't you! I did an awful lot of unsupervised reading," she replied easily. "You'd be amazed at what a girl can learn from the printed word and television. I told him the cops would also look at the husband first if my mother was killed and that I would make sure he stayed in prison for life. I'd testify that they had fights all the time."

"Good God, Marie. He might have killed you for that!"

She nodded. "He threatened that, too, but I presented my insurance. I had a diary, I said. If I died, that plus the evidence would turn up immediately and he'd never find any of it before the police did. I gave him four hours to pack and get out of Atlanta."

Grant couldn't believe a girl that age could manage such a thing. It was a helluva coming of age. He felt speechless.

But the story wasn't over. Marie kept drawing as she told the rest. "So he left. Trouble is, my mother went with him. I spent the next five years with an eighty-year-old woman who lived next door."

Her blue eyes looked old when she faced him again. "We made a deal, Mrs. Cox and I. I would do her errands, keep her independent and out of a nursing home.

She wouldn't rat me out to the authorities, who would have stuck me in foster care. We lived on her Social Security and my paper route."

Grant was shaking his head in disbelief. "What about school?"

"I kept going. Mrs. Cox signed my report cards and wrote excuses when I was absent. I never gave the teachers any reason to contact my parents. Also, I became the ugliest kid in the seventh grade on purpose. Dulled my hair, gained as much weight as I could and never smiled."

"Why? Why on earth did you do that?"

"That was my protection against interference from any quarter. Teachers and counselors looked right through me. Boys didn't bother me. Only when I was through community college did I let myself go blond and smile again. I stopped blacking my teeth and lost thirty pounds. The university met a whole new girl who was prepared for anything and old enough to handle it.

"You blacked your *teeth?*" Grant asked in a near whisper.

She shrugged. "Hey, I figured nobody wants to kiss a girl with rotten teeth." Her grin emphasized their brilliant whiteness now.

Grant tried to smile at her attempt at humor, but he couldn't. He only wished he had known her then. She had needed a friend, someone to defend her.

She would never be without one again if he could help it. "See what you missed by not knowing me back in the day?"

Chapter 12

Grant didn't know what to say. There was no making it right, no matter what he said, but he wished he could tell Marie how much he admired her courage and determination.

"I'm guessing you had a rough time playing with the big boys after you joined the Company, right? Had an even rougher time with that bastard you planned to marry. None of them ever really saw the real you, did they?"

"My choice. I didn't let them," she replied.

He moved closer and sat down next to her on the bed, not caring that she drew back. "It was because they never bothered to scratch the surface. Just like those teachers and counselors."

She laughed a little. "And I suppose you have. I shouldn't have told you all that. Can't imagine why I did."

Grant closed his eyes. "You're a complex woman, Marie. I know there are facets I haven't seen yet. I expect it would take a lifetime. And I'd like to—"

"Stop!" she ordered, and pressed her hand over his, where it rested between them. "Look at me, Grant."

He met her gaze squarely.

"I'm not this defenseless little blonde you have to shelter. That's my cover. I use it when I need to but not right now. This is me: I have a black belt. I'm an expert shot. Even the most seasoned agent can be taken by surprise in an unguarded moment, and that's what happened to me. Not because I'm helpless or incompetent. I did get away from him."

Grant saw her point. "You've been underestimated a lot, and maybe I was guilty of that, too. I admit I'm a little chauvinistic at times."

"You think?" she asked with a wry laugh.

Grant watched her go back to working on the sketch. She had been surprisingly open about her past. That was a good sign, wasn't it? She wanted him to know her.

In all fairness, maybe he ought to let her know him better, too. Maybe that was the key that would open that heart she had locked away so long ago.

He took a deep breath and began. "There was this girl in Germany when I was in ninth grade. Beautiful, blond, small, a lot like you. I was so crazy about her. One day she just up and vanished without a trace. Left everything behind. The Polizei and the Criminal Investigation

Division convinced her family she'd simply run away with some boy, but I knew better."

"Because you were the boy and you didn't have her?"

"No, I had a crush on her, but she barely knew I existed. It's just that she was seventeen, had everything going for her and no reason on earth to run away. She was taken."

"You were sure of that?

He nodded, not adding how hard he had tried to use psychometry to verify it but was never able to get his hands on anything of hers. "I obsessed over it, my not being able to persuade everyone to keep looking for her."

"Any ransom demands?"

"None. There was no word from either her or the kidnapper, and a year later her family rotated back to the States. Everybody just wrote her off."

"Everyone but you. Did you look further after you grew up?"

"Pretty intensively for a couple of years after I graduated. Still no trace," he admitted. "I finally recognized the obsession for what it was, plain old guilt. I figured she was probably dead."

"That must have been hard for you to accept," Marie said, compassion softening her voice.

"It was. Maybe I projected some of her qualities onto you at first. When I first saw your photo in the file, it reminded me of her. You're really nothing like her, of course. Sorry if I—"

"Tried to play knight in shining armor? It's a guy thing, I guess. At least with the nicer guys. Haven't met a lot of those, unfortunately. Don't worry about it."

"I won't. Poor little Betty Schonrock has nothing at all to do with the way I feel about you now. That's all *your* fault."

"Then I'm glad I told you how deviously deadly I can be. Now you know I'm not a wimp."

That was the last thing in the world he'd think. If anything, she was too daring. But what if she hadn't dared? He shuddered to think what might have happened to the child she had been. Or as a woman in that warehouse tied up on a cot and facing only God knew what.

"You're a survivor, that's for sure," he said, feeling an inordinate amount of pride in her resourcefulness, courage and independence.

"Okay! Here he is. What do you think?" she asked, handing Grant her sketchbook.

He took it and laid the side of his palm on the page where her hand had rested.

For a long moment, he didn't even see the picture. The residual energy of hope and yearning she'd left with the sketchbook was so strong it nearly took his breath away.

Beneath all her calculated preparedness, training and determined self-confidence was a little girl desperate for someone to love her and care what happened to her.

She had no earthly reason to believe anyone like that even existed, and he had no way to convince her that he was the one.

His gaze met hers as he looked up from the sketchbook. "You never cease to amaze me, Marie Beauclair."

She tossed her hair and preened comically, making him smile. "You're crushing on me, Tyndal!"

"Like a ninth-grade geek? I'm sort of past that stage, I think." Way past that. This felt more like the real thing.

Marie felt unaccountably good. Maybe Grant was right. She had never told anyone but Mrs. Cox about that episode with her stepfather or her mother's accusation. Even that had been an edited version. She probably shouldn't have told Grant all of it, but at least she'd made her point to him quite clear. She was no victim, and even as a kid she'd proved that. At least to herself.

It bothered her still that she hadn't reported it all to the police, but she'd been bluffing about the evidence and the diary. The most her stepfather would have gotten was a few years in jail, even if she had convinced them she'd been touched inappropriately. She had known that was an iffy proposition.

Well, it was over and maybe she'd scared the man so much he'd never tried it again with anyone else.

Grant had explained his whole attitude with that story about the girl. She wished he'd been able to resolve his early trauma as neatly as she had done her own. What really had happened to little Betty? she wondered.

Grant had gone to interview Pieter's grandfather while she tried to find more information on the Internet about the old clinic. It had been a sanatorium during its last incarnation, as Grant had guessed. No names of staff were included. And no reference to Dr. Shapur there or anywhere else.

The sun was down and it was nearly nine o'clock. Marie logged off, showered quickly and dressed in her dark jeans and black shirt. She pulled her hair back and slipped on her cap. Grant wasn't leaving her behind. She'd wait in the car if necessary, but she was going.

Just as she finished checking her weapon, Grant came in. "Mercier called while I was downstairs. You were right about Shapur. He's Iranian, a physician and a member of the shah's old retinue, ousted in the seventies by the new regime. He disappeared out of Paris shortly after they went into exile there."

"Maybe he came to work for Dr. Shute and just stayed on after the old guy died," Marie guessed.

"Yes, he had a work permit and attained citizenship. The clinic was closed down, and Shute retired in the early nineties, the few patients left moved to a facility in Rotterdam."

"And since then?" Marie asked as Grant began changing his clothes.

"Nothing. Taxes have been paid on the place. That's about it." Grant seemed oblivious to the fact that she was there, watching him. Or maybe he was showing off; she couldn't tell. At any rate she didn't look away. The sight of his bare chest set her hormones dancing, but she stifled the response.

Even as she thought it, he turned and smiled. Marie quickly looked away, determined to focus on the mission, not his spectacular pecs and abs.

"So how do we play it tonight? Park down the road, hoof it to the clinic and sneak in?" she asked.

He paused, obviously thinking about it. She had expected him to jump right on that *we* and make it clear she was to stay out of things. He looked worried but he nodded. "You'll be the lookout, while I gain entry. We'll stay in touch with the ear mics."

"All right!" Marie barely controlled her elation. He was trusting her to participate. She'd had her arguments all ready for him, and now she didn't even need them.

He cleared his throat, then added, "I want you to stay well hidden and keep watch from near the road, where I'll park the car."

Marie gave a grunt of disgust. "Grant! What is it with you? Do you treat the women you work with this way?"

"I haven't worked with women. I told you I work alone," he said evenly, barely a hint of defensiveness in his voice. He pulled on his jacket and fished the car keys out of his pocket.

"It's because I'm a woman, though, isn't it?"

He shrugged one shoulder, an admission of sorts.

"How do you get away with being so chauvinistic?" she demanded, throwing up her hands in frustration.

"I don't know. I'm sorry if it makes you angry."

"It makes me mad as hell! You don't think I'm capable of anything!"

"No, it's not that," he argued, shifting restlessly. "I just can't stand the thought of you getting hurt. Or worse."

She pushed past him and went out the door. "Well, get over it. I'm going in with you, at least up to the house, where I can help if you're outnumbered."

"No. We need someone near the turnoff to keep watch."

"This is not your call."

"It *is* my call! I'm running this op, Marie. You're with me only because of Mercier's insistence, but I can override that if you get in the way!"

They argued all the way downstairs. Pieter met them in front of the desk and stepped in their way. "I couldn't help overhearing." He made a wry face, meant to look ingratiating, which it did, Marie thought. He was cute and he knew it.

"You were loud and I overheard you. Look, I know you are an American agent, sir. Grandfather told me about the badge. Something nefarious is going on at that old clinic he spoke of, isn't it? I would like to be of help."

"Absolutely not," Grant said.

Marie turned to Grant. "He could keep watch by the road."

"We can't involve civilians, Marie. You *know* that," Grant said. "Besides, we don't know what's going on out there. If I had any real evidence that anything was, I would call in the local police. We're only doing reconnaissance at this point."

Pieter straightened his shoulders and raised his chin. "I wasn't always a civilian. I did my military service."

"He qualifies as an agent of opportunity, and we do need another pair of eyes and ears," Marie reminded Grant. "Give him a mic and station him near the turnoff."

"Yes, do!" Pieter insisted. He was obviously hungry for a little excitement in his life.

Grant hesitated, then stared straight into Pieter's eyes. "You have a vehicle?"

"I do. Shall I follow yours?"

"Yes, and follow my directions to the letter. This is a kidnapping we're investigating. More than that I can't divulge. Whatever you see, hear and do must remain confidential or you're liable to international censure, stiff fines and prison. Understood?"

"Yes, sir. Will I need a weapon? I have one."

"Under no circumstances are you to go armed, and I did not hear that admission of owning an illegal firearm."

"Yes, sir. Thank you, sir."

"If you hear any disturbance at all—shots or shouts, any commotion at all—do not approach the conflict. Get back on the main road and call the police immediately. Will you do that?"

"I will. Give me two minutes to get rid of the white shirt and find something dark to wear." He looked over his shoulder at them. "Wait for me!"

Pieter looked like a kid on Christmas morning. Grant looked like a man on death row. "I hope we don't regret this."

"He'll be fine," Marie assured him. "You made his day."

Pieter returned in a flash, dressed all in black, and followed them out to Grant's vehicle, where he was fitted with an ear mic and given instructions on how to operate it. Grant smeared dark cammo paint on his own face, then hers and finally, after a moment's hesitation, he striped Pieter's.

She smiled to herself, liking Grant enormously for that small consideration.

To Marie, Grant snapped, "You get your orders on the way. Let's roll."

She'd just bet she would get orders. Grant had definitely morphed into commando mode. She understood the ramifications of that. He was in charge and she was subordinate. At least in his mind.

Grant quickly dismissed his qualms about letting Pieter come along. It was a done deal, and he'd probably come in handy by warning them if a car approached. Should be safe enough. After all, that's where he had planned to park Marie to keep her out of trouble.

Now he'd have to find a relatively secure place near the clinic to have her hide out and keep watch. It shouldn't take him that long to scout around inside the place and see what he could find.

If they were holding Cynthia Rivers there, he'd find her. If not, maybe he'd discover some clue telling where she was being held. The main thing right now was to get her back alive.

Everybody with a badge was looking for Onders, so he would be captured eventually. Hopefully, he would give up the identity of the other guy, the one who had kidnapped Rivers. Grant was convinced Onders hadn't done that one. The old man was the wild card. How did he fit into this?

Earlier on the phone, Mercier had theorized that the terrorists were using the old doctor as a front and were keeping him alive in case anyone came there to check on the place. He had warned there might be a whole gang of them, but Grant didn't think so.

Forty minutes later Pieter, his old Volvo and Grant's vehicle were secluded in a small grove of trees across the road from the cutoff to the clinic.

Marie didn't object when Grant led her on foot up the

long drive and to the east wing. There, the shrubbery grew high enough for her to stand behind it unobserved. "Stay here," he ordered. "Call me if you see anything out of the ordinary. "We'll rendezvous in one hour or maybe less if I'm successful. If I'm not back by then, phone the police."

"One hour," she affirmed. Then she grasped his forearm. "Be careful, Grant."

"Nice to know you care," Grant said, and dropped a kiss on her war-painted cheek. Then he faded into the night, looking for the best point of entry.

Chapter 13

Marie couldn't stay put. She had to know what was going on inside there. If there were any vehicles on the property, they were closed inside those outbuildings with no windows.

The clinic had windows, though. So many of them. Light spilled out the cracks between the drapes in what must be the main living area. Grant had gone around back. He would be inside by now. She crept to the window and peeked in. The room was empty, but in a few moments she heard voices and the clack of footsteps on the tiles.

She couldn't hear what they were saying, but the tones were angry. When they reached the room she was watching, she recognized Onders immediately.

He was gesturing frantically to the other man, a larger, darker and more menacing version of himself. Now that they were farther inside the room, she could hear them. "Why must I go, too?" They were speaking in Dutch. Onders demanded in a near whine, "You can do this one yourself."

"Brussels is next, and we do it together so there will be no mistakes. The Explorer is repaired?"

"It is. Here are the keys." Onders reached deep into a pocket and came out with a key ring.

"Good. It's settled. Come on. Shapur has cooked for us." They left the living area.

Marie was tempted to go inside, but she remembered Grant's orders. What if she were caught? It could compromise the whole mission.

No doubt she and Grant could take these two down now, but if the two responsible for Cynthia Rivers's kidnapping clammed up at capture or were killed in the process, she might never be found. Maybe Grant would locate the woman and they could wind this up tonight.

Moving like a wraith, Marie left the window and slipped back to the stand of shrubs where Grant had left her. She shielded the dial of the watch he had given her and lighted it to check the time. Ten minutes to rendezvous. She had cut it close.

She heard a slight rustle behind her and crouched, gun drawn.

"It's me," Grant whispered from the shadows. "Come on!"

He darted across the small stretch of lawn that separated the main building from one of the smaller ones.

Moonlight made them vulnerable when out in the open, but she doubted anyone inside was keeping watch. Onders and his friend were probably eating, and she doubted the old doctor could see much past his nose.

Marie stayed low as she ran, noting for the first time that Grant carried someone over his shoulder in a fireman's hold. Rivers, she hoped.

With the outbuilding between them and the clinic, he carefully dumped his burden onto the ground. Then he retrieved a light stick from his pocket and broke it open, providing a low level of illumination.

Marie had expected Cynthia Rivers, but it was the old doctor.

"Why did you make me go with you?" the doctor sputtered. "Who are you?"

"Shh," Grant warned. "Do you know who those men are, Dr. Shapur?"

Shapur nodded as he straightened his old robe, obviously trying to resume what dignity he had left after being treated like a sack of potatoes. "Of course I know. Claude Onders is the grandson of the man who owns the clinic. The other is his partner."

"They're kidnappers," Grant informed him. "We're looking for the young woman one of them kidnapped in Amsterdam yesterday. Did you know they did that?"

Shapur took a few seconds to answer, looking from Grant to Marie and back again before he replied, "I learned of it today, and I was very near finding out where they have put her," Shapur said. "They believe I am senile and partially deaf, so they haven't bothered to guard their words."

"Then she's not here?" Grant demanded, grasping the old man by the shoulder. "You're certain?"

"No, but not far from here, I think." He paused, then added, "They plan to dispose of her on their way to Belgium, so they must have left her somewhere off the road north."

"And they're probably planning to dispose of you before they leave," Grant warned.

"No, no, they have no cause to do that," the doctor argued. "Claude told me earlier that he would return by the weekend with supplies and I should make the place tidy for them."

"You can't trust his word after knowing what he's done!" Marie exclaimed.

The old man smiled, his features ghostly in the meager light. "Oddly enough, I do. He needs me here, you see."

"You're his front," Grant said.

"His what? Oh, yes, I take your meaning." He shook a gnarled finger at Grant. "You should let me go back inside and learn more from them so you can find that young woman. Meanwhile, if they leave, you should follow them and find her."

Marie grabbed Grant's arm and tugged him a few feet away from Shapur. "We need to get him safely away from here."

"*You* get him safely away, back to the road," Grant ordered. "Then drive him back to the hotel. I'll handle those two."

"I'll take him to Pieter, but you wait here for me, Grant. Promise me."

He turned away from her and Marie saw him tense.

"Shapur's gone!" he rasped, throwing up his hands. "Where the hell did he go?"

Marie peeked around the corner of the outbuilding and saw a shadow approaching the side door where Grant must have brought Shapur out. "There! He's going back inside. Man, he moves pretty fast for an old dude! Now what?"

"We hope he's not in on the whole thing. And barring that possibility, pray he doesn't do anything to make them suspicious before they leave. He said they were going to Belgium next?"

"Yeah, that's what I heard them discussing, so that checks out." Too late, she realized she'd given herself away.

"You heard them *when?*" Grant asked, his voice like cold steel.

"I only went around to that window." She pointed. "I didn't go inside." She rushed on, hoping to avoid a tongue-lashing for ignoring his orders. "What I heard verifies what Shapur said, so at least we know the direction they'll take. Like he said, we can follow them when they leave and find Rivers."

"And pray we can get to her before they kill her," Grant said.

"So we simply wait?"

"Well, a showdown's not practical. There are too many places between here and the Belgian border that Cynthia Rivers could be stashed. She might die before anyone discovers where she is." He sighed. "And there's Shapur to consider, too, now that he's back in there with them. I just hope the old boy's trustworthy. How did he seem to you?"

"Fairly bright. We know he's an opportunist, living on Dr. Shute's property, probably catering to the grandson so he can stay here rent-free. He must have some deal with him to look after the place."

Grant hummed in assent. "He seemed almost too cooperative, though, if that's the case. I wonder if he's thought about where he'll go and what he'll do after Onders is arrested."

Marie kept watch on the house. "You don't think he'd give them a heads up, do you? I mean, he's got to know we haven't called in the locals about this or they'd be here already. And you didn't even tell him we're agents."

"No, as far as he knows, we're just here to rescue Cynthia Rivers."

"Maybe we ought to go in after them now in case he's in cahoots."

Marie liked that Grant thought about that for a minute before responding and didn't automatically shoot down the suggestion. "Let's wait and see what happens next. If he tells them we're out here, either they'll come looking for us or they'll run."

Marie finished the thought. "Or he won't tell them and they'll head for Belgium by way of wherever they left Rivers." She kept her eyes on the clinic. "You're right, we should wait, but I think we should go back to the car and do that. There's only one way off the property. They can't go through the fields because of the irrigation ditches."

"That means we have to trust Shapur to take care of himself. However, if they decide to get rid of him, we can't save him anyway unless we take them down now."

"Our choice is between ensuring his safety when he might not even need us or sticking with the possibility of saving Rivers. I say we let him handle them. He's done okay so far."

"Let's go wait with the car, then," Grant said. "You first and stay close to the hedge."

They ran single file down the driveway until they reached the grove of trees where Pieter waited with both vehicles.

"What is happening?" he asked, his voice pitched high with excitement.

"We're going to follow the kidnappers when they leave," Grant told him. "When we do, I want you to return to Gouda."

"Shall I go to the police and alert them?"

"No!" Grant and Marie answered in unison. Then Grant explained. "We stand a much better chance of recovering the victim if we don't have an armed posse breathing down our necks. You do as I tell you. Go back and wait for us at the hotel."

"Yes, sir," Pieter said, obviously disappointed at being cut out of the loop before things popped.

Marie felt a little sorry for him. "Surveillance is tedious, but it's very important, Pieter. We needed you stationed out here tonight, and you did an excellent job of it."

"Surveillance! Yes, I can say I did that, can't I?"

"You certainly can, and you'll get full credit for helping with the mission," she told him. "Now what you have to do is wait until their vehicle and ours are completely out of sight, then leave, okay? You don't want to alert them."

He nodded succinctly, shoulders straight. "Affirmative."

Marie smiled to herself. Did she know how to handle men or what? Grant nudged her and told her to get in the car.

Forty minutes later headlights appeared, coming down the driveway.

"Showtime," she muttered.

Grant watched the car turn left onto the highway. Waiting until it was nearly out of sight, he then pulled out of concealment and followed with the headlights off. Marie waved to Pieter, who returned the salute.

"I hope he follows orders better than you do," Grant said. "He's seen way too many Bond movies."

"Give him a break, Grant. Don't you remember how thrilling you thought it would be just before you became an agent?"

"I guess. Nobody bothered to tell me it would mostly involve sitting around waiting for something to happen, spending hours doing prep and background work."

"Then there's the gadding about European countries with fellow agents, like *now*," Marie added with a laugh. "Yeah, such boring work. We should have become accountants."

"With my math grades? Not really an option."

She laughed again. "Seriously, do you like the job?"

"As of this afternoon, I seriously love it."

"Keep your mind on the mission, Tyndal. We're in pursuit, in case you forgot."

He shifted gears. "I'm with it. I just meant that when

all things come together, the blood's pumping and you get down to the wire on a case, it's all I envisioned. You, too?"

She blew out a sigh. "Well, I haven't actually had that much excitement until Onders grabbed me. Before that, it was mostly sneaking around, plundering through people's desks during parties, eavesdropping, planting bugs, that sort of thing. A bit nerve-racking a time or two when I nearly got caught, but not all that dangerous. Nobody took me seriously enough to credit I was a spy even if I had been discovered."

"The dizzy blonde impression is a dynamite cover. You even had me fooled."

"And now you realize I'm wise as Solomon and can be trusted to handle any situation? Get real, Tyndal. You *still* think I'm a cupcake."

"Sweet as one, I'll admit."

"Shut up," she muttered, then tensed. "Look, they're slowing down. Turning?"

"Looks like it." He cut the lights and decelerated. "Yep, there they go."

Grant turned, too. Clouds were obscuring the moonlight now and made it impossible to see the road. Minutes later he lost the illumination the car lights ahead had provided. "Where are their damn lights?"

"Maybe they reached their destination?" Marie guessed. She propped one palm against the dash and leaned forward as if that would help her to see.

Grant had slowed to a crawl when all of a sudden, high headlights appeared behind them. "Is that Pieter?" Grant growled. "I'll wring his neck!"

Suddenly the trailing car roared forward and they

were rammed from behind. Grant struggled to keep control, propelled forward by a much larger force. Marie fought the passenger side air bag, which had deployed. Grant lucked out when his failed.

"It'll collapse. Don't panic!" he shouted over the grind of metal and roar of engines.

They hit the car ahead of them hard and came to an abrupt stop, sandwiched between the two vehicles. He quickly popped his seat belt and saw that Marie was out of hers. "You okay?" he demanded as he slid as low in the seat as possible.

"Uh-huh." She had her weapon in hand and was checking the load.

"When somebody shows, fire at will," Grant said, hoping that whoever did this wouldn't riddle the car with bullets before checking things out. He didn't think they would, since all three vehicles were so close that they could damage theirs and be stranded.

For a long moment nothing happened. Grant wished he could shield her, but her lower half was wedged in the floorboard. She braced her weapon and aimed at the passenger side window.

He leaned sideways into the passenger seat, his Glock close to his chest and pointing at the driver's-side window.

"Get out of the car!" a loud voice demanded in English.

Grant and Marie remained silent.

There was a scuffling sound outside the car, then voices. "Maybe they're unconscious. Or dead." This time, the words were in Dutch. Marie whispered a translation.

"Torch it," the first voice suggested. Grant understood that much.

"That could draw attention from the highway. There's no way out of here but the road in. Besides, we need to see who we have. What if it's only one of them?"

Marie whispered again, "They're approaching. Get ready."

A form appeared at her window, but she didn't fire. Grant realized she was waiting for the other one to show. The headlights from the rear vehicle threw light through their back window, but he and Marie were in shadow.

All of a sudden, the driver's door flew open and Grant opened fire. Marie's weapon discharged not a foot from his head, deafening him. He could feel the discharge of gunpowder, hot on his face.

His weapon bucked repeatedly, and he stopped just before emptying it of the last three shots. He had to have hit something out there.

Without pause, he sprang upward and slid sideways out the driver's door, landing on the ground. A body lay sprawled, arms outflung. He scooped up the dead man's weapon as he scrambled up and threw himself over the trunk of his vehicle to the opposite side. A figure was running, headed for the nearby trees.

"Marie?" he called.

"Get him!" she shouted from somewhere behind him. Grant raised his Glock and fired the last three.

The runner fell.

He glanced back at the car and saw Marie climbing out of it. "You hurt?" he asked, and saw her raise her head and say something. She looked okay. "Marie?"

She ran over to him. "I'm fine. Were you hit?"

"No. My ears are still ringing but otherwise I'm okay."

"Thank God."

"Reload and stay here," he ordered, motioning for good measure in case her hearing was affected, too. Grant got a flashlight out of the car and hurried over to where the second man had fallen to see whether he had survived. He hadn't.

"This is the one I saw through the window talking with Onders," Marie said.

With a feeling of dejection, Grant picked up the body, slung it over his shoulder and returned to where Marie waited with the other body. He flopped the kidnapper onto the ground at her feet.

"Onders," she observed with a fatalistic frown.

"Dead," he said, without adding what they both knew.

Cynthia Rivers wouldn't stand much of a chance now. The men who knew where she was wouldn't be telling anyone.

Chapter 14

Grant knelt and searched pockets. No identification on Onders. He motioned to the SUV that had hit them from the rear, and Marie went to search it while Grant checked out the other body and the car in front of them.

He was looking in the trunk when he heard her shout. "Passports!" She waved them out the window.

Grant gave her a thumbs-up and approached her with the sleeve of paperwork he'd found in the first vehicle. They inspected it in the dome light. Title and registration papers, unfamiliar names. No surprise there. No particular energy emanating from them, either, he noted.

"Same for this one. Fake names," she said, "and their passports match."

She got out and headed for the first car. "We should

go up the road and see what's there just in case they actually were going there to get rid of Rivers."

Grant didn't hold much hope for that, but he agreed. They got in the kidnappers' car and drove to the dead end, where a burned-out farmhouse lay in ruin. Its chimney stood like a squat lonely guard over what had once been someone's home.

"Maybe they set fire to it with her in the house," Marie commented.

"No. Look at the weeds. The fire was several weeks ago, at least. She's not here."

They turned around and drove back to the scene of the shooting. "We have to call the police," Grant said.

"Wait," Marie said. "There's Shapur. We need to pick him up before he gets away. He set this up, Grant, a clear case of attempted murder. Chances are excellent that he knows all about the kidnappings. He might even be the one who arranged them."

"Let's go. Back that SUV out of the way and let's see if ours will still run."

It wouldn't. Grant transferred his equipment from the trunk, they climbed into the SUV, and the pair headed back to the clinic.

Marie had grown deathly quiet. Grant worried that she was dwelling on the shooting. "You didn't kill him, Marie," he told her. "I fired the fatal shots."

She blew out a sigh. "It's not that. It just bothers me that I was so ready to do it. I wanted him dead, both of them. Even knowing what was at stake, a young woman's life, I shot to kill." Her voice sounded a little teary, but she was holding it together.

"Training plus instinct," he explained. "You had no clear shot to wound, and you knew it was them or us. It *was,* Marie. They were there for no other reason than to get rid of us, and you know that. Don't second-guess your decision. It'll slow you down the next time and could cost your or your partner's life. You *must* trust your instincts."

"We have to find her, Grant. That poor woman does not deserve to die alone and terrified."

Grant didn't point out that they couldn't save everyone, that some died in spite of the fact that they did their best, prayed their hardest and shot their straightest.

He had learned that the hard way when leading his navy team on what often amounted to suicide missions. Every death that occurred due to his orders or actions, deserved or otherwise, felt like a gaping wound in his soul. Maybe he would have done better as an accountant, but then he wouldn't have saved the ones he did save.

"We just do everything we can, Marie, and hope it's enough."

The clinic appeared dark when they returned. Marie wondered if Shapur had left, too. Perhaps he was in the back, in the kitchen area where lights wouldn't be visible from the front.

Grant didn't make any attempt to conceal their approach. They were, after all, driving the kidnappers' SUV. The element of surprise would come when they were face-to-face with him.

The old structure looked eerie, a ghostly shade of blue in the light of the moon. Clouds still drifted overhead, periodically casting the place in moon shadow. "This place is really spooky," she commented.

"Just now noticing that?" he asked.

"Well, we were a little busy before. Looks like something out of a fifties film noir, doesn't it?"

Grant hummed an answer as he parked near the front. They drew their weapons and got out. "We need to secure Shapur, then scout the rest of the place," he said. "Rivers might be concealed somewhere on the premises other than the main building."

"I just hope they didn't kill her before they left."

Grant tilted his head to one side as if considering. "They wouldn't if the ransom hasn't been denied. And if Shapur is running the show, which is a fair bet, since he sent them after us, he would have the final say."

"How do you want to handle it? Do we confront him immediately or let him keep pretending and see what he does? Maybe he'll give her up if he thinks we don't suspect him."

Grant threw out his arm and stopped her on the walkway as they approached the front door. "Something's not right," he said in a low voice. She heard his deep intake of breath and rapid exhale.

He had brought the flashlight with him for the search and flashed it on the door. Suddenly, he dropped it, grasped her arm and ran, dragging her with him. Marie stumbled.

He scooped her up and jumped over something. Then he pushed her down behind the low stone wall that surrounded the gravel drive and threw himself on top of her.

"Cover your head," he warned as he did it.

The horrific explosion lit up the night, the concussion enormous. Debris rained all over them.

When it stopped, Marie struggled, but he held her there, his arm like a vise around her middle, his body covering the length of hers, his face buried in the curve where her neck met her shoulder. *Deadweight.*

"Grant! Can you move? Let me up!" she cried, praying he *could* move, that he wasn't injured or, worse, dead. He had saved her life, thrown himself between her and disaster without a thought for his own safety. What kind of man did that?

He groaned, rolled off her and lay on his back, one arm covering his eyes. "Lord, that was *way* too close!"

"Are you all right? Are you hurt?" she asked frantically. She quickly propped herself up on her elbow as she lay on her side next to him and ran her hand over his face.

He caught her hand in his, pressed her palm to his lips for several seconds. "I almost lost you," he growled, slid his arms around her and drew her on top of him.

The kiss grew fervent, more desperate than sexual. She felt his heart thundering beneath hers and reveled in the fact that they had both survived. She kissed him back, tasting the waning fear and relief they shared.

He broke the kiss and framed her face with his hands, looking into her eyes, searching. "I love you, Marie. I should have said it before. I knew it before but didn't want to scare you off. What if we'd been blasted to kingdom come and I had never said those words?"

She couldn't speak. Hope flared, choking off speech, even if she had known what to say. Flickers of a future with him ran through her brain like a film on fast-forward. Loving, laughing, living without the constant loneliness she had always accepted as normal for her.

Then reason intruded and it dawned on her that this was simply an adrenalin-inspired declaration. Like the kiss, just a life-affirming thing, a glad-to-be-alive connection.

What could she say that wouldn't sound dismissive or ungrateful? That she loved him, too? No. If she said that, the words wouldn't be coming from the same place as his. She was afraid she would really mean it.

He brushed the hair off her brow with one finger, then pulled a small packet of wipes out of his pocket and began cleaning the dirt and dark greasepaint off her face.

Marie remained motionless as he tended to her, thinking how gentle he could be at times. And how she both resented and welcomed being treated like something too precious to risk. She couldn't have it both ways. Could she?

"It's okay whatever you're thinking. You don't have to say anything back. I just wanted you to know," he said softly. "I had to tell you."

That little mind-movie he had triggered scared her. She wanted all that way too much, and wanting anything so desperately always led to disappointment.

Marie took a deep breath and closed her eyes. She pushed off him and sat up. "So what the hell *was* that? A bomb?"

"Gas explosion," he replied as he sat up, too, and began scrubbing his own face with one of the skimpy wipes, missing several spots.

She took the wipe out of his hand and finished the

job for him. "So, you really *are* psychic. Sorry I ever doubted you."

He ran a hand through his hair, then ruffled it to dislodge the debris that had peppered him. "Well, not in this instance, I wasn't. I smelled the gas as we approached. The doorbell would have set it off."

"But we didn't ring it, so something else set it off. What?"

"Shapur must have called it in. A ringing phone would set it off. Guess he saw us coming."

"So where is he now?" She looked around, as if she could find him with all the places he could be hiding. No way.

"He could be anywhere."

Marie looked at the ruined building. "What if Rivers was in there?"

"I searched all the rooms on both floors before I brought Shapur out. If she is here, she has to be in a basement or one of the outbuildings."

"Let's go look." Marie was already on her feet and headed for the clinic, most of which was still standing with a gaping hole where the front portal had been, windows blown out and huge portions of the roof missing.

The explosion had triggered fire, and lazy flames were licking out the doorways in the exposed hallway. Marie quickened her steps. "Come on—we need to hurry in case she's under all that."

"Wait." He grabbed her arm. "Let's go around back to enter. If there's a basement, the entrance to it will probably be in or near the kitchen."

He was all business now, she noted. Hard-edged, no-

nonsense, agent-in-charge. Whispered avowals and heated kisses forgotten already.

Despite the way she had skirted the personal issue, she obviously wasn't as nimble as he was when it came to switching mind gears.

She would never figure him out, never be able to guess what he'd do next or plan how she would react. Total surrender of control was not something she could handle, even if she did happen to fall in love with him. And that was all too likely to happen if she didn't hurry up and break all ties, physical and emotional.

Maybe it was too late already.

The problem was with her and she knew it. No way could she ever fall for a weak-willed, easily led man; yet neither could she abide one who thought he could own her, body and soul.

Grant already treated her as if he needed to watch her every move and make all the decisions for her.

"Stay behind me and keep your eyes open," he ordered, proving her point with alacrity.

"And if I don't?" she snapped.

"Then I won't have anyone watching my back. What's gotten into you all of a sudden?"

Okay, now she was letting her emotions override her good sense and training. He simply upset all her priorities and threatened every goal she had ever set for herself.

This was not the time for a personal altercation between the two of them, however. They had work to do and had to do it together with utmost efficiency. A life was at stake.

"I'll watch your back," she agreed.

Grant knew he had pushed too far too soon. Marie was backing off as if he'd issued a threat instead of admitting he loved her. No wonder, since she must feel they barely knew each other. Well, he knew enough whether she did or not.

He had made a serious error by telling her this and couldn't think of any way to fix it.

A loud groan snagged his attention, and he froze, glancing around the littered back garden. The force of the blast had blown out the back door and windows. Shutters lay scattered and splintered among the flowering plants and bushes. "Over there!" he said, pointing toward a stone bench several yards away.

Marie was already headed there. "It's the doctor!" she announced, dropping to her knees beside the prone figure.

Grant joined her, shining the flashlight on the man to see the extent of his injuries. A long splinter of wood, a good two inches in diameter, protruded from his side and blood seeped out around it.

Grant fished out his cell phone and quickly called the emergency number for an ambulance.

"Where is Cynthia Rivers?" Marie demanded. She must realize the old man might not last until the medics arrived and she was taking care of business.

Grant could almost feel her effort to deny sympathy and comfort. They had to find that woman, and Shapur was their last chance to get the location.

"I—I don't know," Shapur insisted. A trickle of red escaped the corner of his mouth. Punctured lung, Grant thought, and maybe worse.

"Could she be here in one of the outbuildings?" Marie demanded. "Are you certain she's not on the premises?"

Shapur gave a negative shake of his head, barely a recognizable movement. "No, not certain." He grasped Marie's wrist. "Saw their auto. I thought you were them."

"You caused the explosion," Grant stated.

Shapur nodded. "Knew they would come back. They must think the money…" His eyes closed, but he spoke again. "Is in the safe." His gnarled fingers clawed at his side. "The number…an account. Take it to Bahktar."

"A place or a name?" Grant asked.

"He will be in Paris. Give it to him. Please…save my child. In the name of…goodness."

"What child? What do you mean?" Marie asked, her voice going soft with concern Grant knew she couldn't help but have. The man was dying and he was worried about his child.

"Daughter." Shapur sighed out the word. "I was forced out of Iran with my shah."

"You were the shah's physician?"

Again a shake of the head. "Consulting. I was at the palace when…"

"Okay, okay, got that," Marie said quickly. "What about the child?"

"She is there still. Tehran. Mamud Bahktar will have her killed if…denied the ransoms I collected for him."

"So, he set this up through you, using extortion?" Grant asked. "Is he with the current regime in Iran?"

"An agent for the…Republican Guard. Hates Americans, Brits, Israelis."

"And the money is for arms, right?"

Shapur nodded. "Hezbollah."

"They want a bigger foothold on the West Bank, Gaza Strip. You know we can't allow him to fund that, Shapur," Grant said. "Not even to save your daughter."

"I'm sorry about your child," Marie murmured, laying her hand on the man's shoulder.

"Who is a grown woman, at least thirty- or forty-something," Grant declared. "The shah was ousted in seventy-nine, Marie. This man is responsible for the death of at least one American woman who was a lot younger than his daughter."

"No! Not murder!" Shapur's shout ended in a gurgle as blood flowed from his mouth. "And not Claude. The other…"

"His name?" Grant prompted.

"De Lange. Jarig De Lange," Shapur gasped.

"Dutch like Onders? You hired them here?"

Shapur coughed, fought for breath and lost the battle.

Marie's fingertips pressed the doctor's carotid. "He's gone." She sat flat on the ground and pressed the heel of her hand to her forehead.

Grant laid his hand on her shoulder and gave it a squeeze of comfort. "Don't waste your grief on him. He wasn't worth it. He sent Onders and De Lange after us to kill us. And he set off that explosion to get rid of them when he thought they had come back. Look how he's dressed."

Shapur had changed clothes. He wore slacks, a shirt, jacket and dress shoes. Grant searched the body and found keys along with a wallet full of Euros and a passport. He handed those to Marie and kept the key ring.

"When the cops get here, do not turn those items over to anyone," he warned.

"He was leaving," Marie said, staring at the passport. "There must be another vehicle in one of the outbuildings."

"He'd have made it, too, if that sliver of board from the explosion hadn't impaled him." Grant had the keys clutched tightly, feeling the energy trapped in them. "He was going to kill this Bahktar he mentioned." He began searching the garden around them for a travel bag.

"There it is," he muttered, hurrying over to a small weekend bag. He flipped it open and found nothing but a change of clothes and toiletries.

No weapon apparent, but the doctor would use something subtle and easily concealed like drugs or poison. Grant clutched the shaving kit and could feel further determination, hatred and absolute conviction that it could be done. *Shapur's energy, captured in the planning phase of a killing.* He would probably get more from the wallet if he had the time, but this would get them started.

"He planned to off this Mamud Bahktar when he met him in Paris. With Onders and De Lange out of the way and Bahktar dead, all his problems would go away. He could keep the money he'd amassed from the ransoms, and no one would have been the wiser."

Marie looked up from the body. "He was trying to save his daughter's life, Grant. Wouldn't you have done almost anything if you were him?"

"Maybe," Grant admitted with a shrug. "Yeah, probably. But greed played a part. He planned to keep the money."

"Maybe he would have used it to get his daughter out

of Iran. I hate that he died." She shifted position, moving as if she were suddenly weary of everything. "Even if he was as evil as Satan, he was our best hope of finding Cynthia Rivers."

"We're not giving up," Grant stated, tossing the keys up and catching them in his fist. "Let's go look for her. She must be here somewhere."

He heard the singsong of sirens. "Here comes the cavalry. I guess we'll be tied up for a while answering questions, but at least we'll have plenty of help looking for Cynthia."

"Then what?" Marie asked. "We aren't done, are we?"

Grant slipped an arm around her and pulled her close. "Do you want to be?"

"No," she said with a sigh, relaxing against him and then easing out of his grasp. "What I want to do is find our victim and then go to Paris after that terrorist. What did you get from handling Shapur's things?"

"Enough." Grant smiled. She was acting skittish, but that few seconds hesitation before she had pulled away told him she'd had to think about doing it. It hadn't been an automatic withdrawal. She needed him but didn't want to seem weak. Or too easily had. Maybe she was stronger in a lot of ways than he was.

Chapter 15

"You ever been to Paris?" Grant asked Marie, hoping to lighten the situation and give her a chance to regroup before the cops got there. The last couple of hours had been pretty intense.

"No. Have you?"

"First trip. You'll have to memo another map."

"Not a problem," she said, sounding distracted. "But first we have to help find Cynthia."

She stood and turned as the sirens grew loud. The police cars and an ambulance were rolling up the drive from the main road with lights flashing.

The interrogations were lengthy and tedious, first taking place on-site and then again at the police station. The search, delayed by the necessity of removing rubble, lasted well into the next afternoon. And not a trace of Cynthia Rivers was anywhere to be found, either inside the clinic or on the estate.

To further complicate matters, Grant and Marie were ordered not to leave Gouda until the investigation was complete. The authorities were keeping the incident out of the papers, but it was only a matter of time before it broke.

"When this hits the airwaves, Bahktar will disappear while we hang around here doing nothing," Marie said when they were back in their hotel room.

"You still have the wallet and passport?"

She reached inside her jacket pocket and handed them over. There had been no moment of privacy to examine them once the police had arrived.

Grant carefully removed and studied every paper enclosed in the wallet. "Pay dirt!" he whispered as he grinned at Marie and handed her a slip of paper with a seven-digit number and an abbreviation. The partial name of a bank and a numbered account.

Grant whipped out his phone. "Bahktar can't get his ransom money without the number of the account that Shapur put it in. And we have that."

"What sort of feeling do you get about this Bahktar guy?" She glanced at the wallet. "From handling that."

"Nothing more than Shapur told us. He was straight about that." Grant felt a further connection to Marie now. She was fully on board with the trust thing, at least when it came to business matters. Personal trust would come soon if he could make himself be patient.

He reached over and kissed her on the cheek as he

waited for Mercier to answer his call. She didn't seem to mind, even giving him a little half smile that almost showed dimples. But the reticence was still there.

"Tyndal?" Mercier snapped out his name first thing, probably wondering why he'd gotten only the basic, readily obtainable facts pertaining to the incident. He'd be wanting impressions, whatever details weren't supported by the available evidence, Marie's actions and reactions. And definitely Grant's next plan of action. The locals had been ever present and had kept Grant too busy to give a full report.

"Hi, boss," Grant said. "You want to get us permission to leave Holland or wait a few days and ask forgiveness? We're about to defy the powers that be."

"What else is new?" Mercier asked.

"Hey, I've been as cooperative as I could be under the circumstances. Right by the rule book. Your book, anyway."

"That's not what I meant," Mercier said, impatience obvious. "I mean, literally, what else is *new?*"

"Oh, well, we're off to Paris. Driving. I have the account number, and there's an Iranian there waiting to get the funds. Name's Mamud Bahktar. Look him up, please, all sources, and give us whatever you find before we set up a meeting. It's a real long shot, but I'm hoping Shapur mentioned to him where the girl was being held. Because of that, we'll go in soft and see what we can get before we nail him."

"I'll get everybody on it right away and see what we can find. Stay at the safe house." He gave an address. "Anything else you need?"

"I need phone records for the clinic if you could get those. I think the doctor only had the landline, since Onders phoned to one when he called Shapur from Amsterdam, but check for a cell. Bahktar's number would be helpful. His is almost surely a cell. Also we need an empath to help find Rivers."

"Vinland's already on his way to Amsterdam. He's the best we've got. How's our new prospect working out?"

"Marie? She's been a godsend. Sharp as a tack. Perfect choice for the team."

"Why am I sensing a decided lack of objectivity, Tyndal? That's pretty flowery praise coming from a man who prefers to work alone. You're not—"

"Shutting her out? Tried that, but she wouldn't let me. She's very involved in the case, sir. Huge help. Give us a buzz when you get that info on Bahktar. Thanks." Grant clicked off before Mercier could ask anything else.

There were probably rules somewhere in Mercier's book about intimate fraternization among the troops, especially highly prized, would-be troops. Couldn't be helped in this case.

Grant wanted a solid commitment from Marie before they hit the States. Then, if it came down to the job or the relationship, Grant figured he would find something else to do. His priorities were pretty much set in concrete at this point, and she was right up there at the top.

"Thanks for the buildup," she said. "You really want me to go for it, don't you?"

"Perfect for you, just like I said, and the pay's a lot better."

She crossed her arms and tilted her head, looking

at him through those long, gold-tipped lashes. "And the benefits?"

"Definitely better," he said with a wink.

She pursed her lips and shrugged. "We'll see about that."

Maybe she was coming around. If she were averse to continuing what they had started, she would have said so, wouldn't she?

"We'll have to keep it platonic, the way we first planned. The way you promised," she said as she began to pack her things in her bag.

"Hey, wait a minute…"

"I know, I know. I was the instigator, but it was a mistake. We both know that."

Well, damn. Grant hid his frustration as well as he could. "If you say so. Personally, I don't see it that way and I don't regret it at all."

"I guess that's your stab at a compliment," she replied, "so I'll take it as one."

"You are pretty fantastic, just so you know."

"Drop it. We don't have time for this," she snapped.

"Okay. Whatever you say."

He didn't need to remind her that she was the one who initiated things and released him from his promise. She had just taken full responsibility for that, even though he certainly hadn't discouraged her in any way. He should accept half the blame for it at least, but he had a feeling that would be the wrong thing to say at this point.

Marie *did* want him; he knew that. But she didn't want to want him. She surely wouldn't want to love him or hear again that he loved her. It was just too soon.

The woman had some heavy baggage to unload. Maybe he did, too. It seemed to him he was having to constantly reevaluate where they were going and how they were going to get there. Or if they were.

Their physical destination was a given, though, and it was time they got on the road to Paris.

As for their emotional direction, he had no available map. Unless Marie had a map of her own in that amazing brain of hers and was just leading him on a merry chase for the hell of it, they were both wandering around in the dark.

"We should have flown," Marie grumbled. Road trips were not her favorite thing, especially at night, when she couldn't see any sights, and when somebody else was behind the wheel and in complete charge of the excursion.

"Lighten up," Grant said. "It's not a long way. Just sit back and enjoy the ride."

The last border crossing from Belgium into France had been a test of patience. They had encountered two new guards who were obviously out to justify their jobs. She'd been afraid the Dutch police would have issued an All Points Bulletin on them already.

With Pieter's help, they had sneaked out the back exit of the hotel and borrowed his car, a vintage Passat that reminded her of the old Volvo Grant had driven to Holland.

"Trust me, we'll probably save time going by car if you count the wait at the airports, time spent renting a car and everything," Grant said. "Less than three hundred klicks to go now. What's the matter? Don't you like Pieter's car?"

She groaned. "You have a real thing for antiques, don't you?"

"It's only twelve years old," he stated. "I get that you like sporty and small, but this one's solid. Heavy and well balanced." He bumped the heel of his hand on the steering wheel.

"Clunky and ugly," she declared. "Just like that thing you rented in Germany."

"Sorry, this is the only vehicle we could take that wouldn't be missed by the cops and Pieter was still eager to help. Vicarious thrill for him, I guess."

"Pity he didn't have a Porsche."

"You'll get your little 'roller skate' back soon, don't worry. You can have it shipped home and wow all your friends."

"Assuming I go back to the States."

He didn't reply. Marie supposed he was giving her space to make up her own mind about COMPASS. Nothing he'd said since mentioning the *benefits* had anything to do with persuading her.

She found herself wanting to go, maybe see him often and see what developed. Ha. Developments so far had done nothing but shake up all her preconceptions and addle her already wobbly composure. She had blown her cover where he was concerned. He knew her all too well, and that made her wary.

"I'm not good being myself," she muttered, shocked that she'd actually said it out loud.

"That must have been hard to admit. Have I met the real you yet?" He smiled over at her; she returned the smile in spite of herself.

She liked him so much. Too much. What a problem to have. "What you see is what you get, I guess. I'm too exhausted to role-play."

"Then I like who I see. Unpretentious, comfortable with casual, honest and open. Smart. Yeah, I noticed that." He cocked his head to one side. Was he baring his jugular, daring her to strike? "You don't pretend much with me anymore, do you?"

"Not much. You did take me for a victim at first. I played that up and let you. But I'm not, and I hope you know that now."

"You made it pretty clear," he agreed with a nod. "How about when we went to the consulate about Rivers? That a role?"

"Docile agent. That's my biggest stretch."

"Worked well," he said. "So what about when we…?"

Marie couldn't lie. "All me, unfortunately."

"No pretense at all?" he insisted.

"I had checked my brain at the front door—what can I say?"

Grant laughed. "You sure hate losing control, don't you?"

"Hey, I *was* in control! Maybe I wasn't thinking too straight, but I was—"

"Physically on top of the situation," he finished for her. "Guess I'm not macho enough to mind that. Kind of loved it, if you want the truth."

She crossed her arms over her chest and frowned down at her knees. "Don't talk about it."

"Why not? Does it make you nervous? Don't tell me you're a prude!"

"It sounds as if you're discussing what we had for lunch or something."

"Did it mean more to you than that? It did to me," he confessed. "I'm not making light of it, but it did happen and I'm not about to forget it."

"And let me guess, you'd like for it to happen again," she said with a mirthless laugh.

"Wouldn't you?"

"I don't know. Don't back me into a corner, Tyndal."

He fanned his fingers above the steering wheel. "Sorry. I said anything you want and I meant that. You know you can trust me."

Could she? Marie wondered. He had proved trustworthy so far. She could actually sleep in the same room with him without keeping one eye open. He had saved her life at the clinic. Why not admit how secure he made her feel, even though she knew she could take care of herself?

"What is it that bothers you about me?" he asked. When she merely shot him a quelling look, he insisted. "Really, I'm interested to know, and I'll change it if I can."

"You hover," she said honestly. "It gives me the feeling that you think I'm incompetent."

His brow furrowed while he digested that.

"I'm not a china doll that chips or breaks at the least little stress, Grant. You need to give me some credit. And telling your boss how great I am doesn't count. For all I know, you just want me to get the job so it will be convenient for us to hook up occasionally."

"Oh," he said finally. That shut him up, which she thought had been her intention. Oddly though, she felt disappointed that he didn't protest and try to talk his way around the accusation. Was it true?

They rode in silence for a good ten minutes before he cleared his throat and shifted a little in his seat. Marie readied herself for the argument to come.

"I'd kill for a cup of coffee. Want to stop?"

She had to realign her thoughts and it took a second. "All right."

"Then you can drive the rest of the way. I'd rather stick pins in my eyes than drive in Paris."

"I thought you'd never been there."

"I haven't, but I've heard horror tales from everyone who has. You handle it."

"Oh, great, a sop to my ego. Just what I wanted."

"You're a hard woman to please," he said with a grin. "I guess I need more practice."

Marie wondered how long he would keep trying. He would never really change. No matter what he said, he'd never see her any other way than as the weak little woman who needed a big strong man to stand guard and fight all her battles. She had given him that false first impression on purpose, but he should have seen past that by now.

Unless he saw *all* women that way.

Chapter 16

They exited the motorway at Baupaume to tank up and buy a map. Grant located a sidewalk café still open where they ordered coffee and a late supper. Marie unfolded the map and studied it as they took a break. "It's the middle of tourist season, and we don't have reservations. Paris will be mobbed."

"Not a problem. The teams keep a safe house just off of Rue Saint Jacques. I don't know of any ongoing ops in Paris right now, but if anyone's using it, they'll have to share—Mercier's orders."

He leaned close to look at the map so that his face was only inches from hers. "It's supposed to be on the left bank near the Sorbonne." He tapped the map. "Here."

"I hope it has two bedrooms."

He didn't reply to that at all. He just kept studying the map.

Marie wondered if she had hurt his feelings. So far he hadn't done a thing to offend her. She had come on to him or he would never have had sex with her. And that certainly hadn't been offensive in any way. It was herself she didn't trust in the same bedroom with him, but she hadn't made it sound that way.

"If you're too tired, I'll drive," he said when they approached the car.

"Now you're spoiling your grand gesture. Give me the keys."

They rode in silence, Marie concentrating on the road, Grant napping in the passenger seat. Or was he pouting? She'd never seen a man pout before, so she wasn't sure. It seemed out of character for a guy like him. He was usually right up front about everything, sometimes a little too frank.

Whatever he was doing, it lasted until they reached Paris. When she exited onto Rue de la Chappelle, he woke up. "That was quick."

"No, it wasn't!" She gritted her teeth as she dodged in and out of traffic, maneuvering a vehicle larger than most of the others on the streets.

The close calls made her glad she wasn't driving her own car. It was smaller and a lot easier to handle, but she couldn't imagine getting out of town without a few dents in whatever she was driving.

"I should have stayed on the autoroute around the city and exited from the south."

"Why didn't you?" Grant asked.

She gave a nervous little laugh as she navigated an unexpected roundabout. "Considering how little I saw of Amsterdam, I thought this might be my only chance to see the city sights. What a joke! I can't take my eyes off the street for a second!"

"If you pass anything interesting, I'll describe it to you." Grant seemed perfectly composed, not the least bit nervous about her driving. He had to be faking that, Marie thought. She was a wreck already, and they still had three-fourths of the city to get through. "You conned me into driving, didn't you?"

"Yeah," he admitted with a dry little laugh.

The map in her head was clear enough, but she made a number of wrong turns simply because she couldn't find an opening in traffic to change lanes. Lanes were a joke here anyway. She cursed under her breath and banged the steering wheel when a taxi cut her off and zoomed past.

"Finally!" she huffed when she made it to Rue Saint Jacques.

"Go left," Grant ordered, and quickly located the building and chose a spot to park the car. Marie followed directions and didn't even think about protesting. She was too exhausted.

Grant got out, purposely didn't open her door for her and grabbed their bags out of the back. He watched Marie as she joined him on the sidewalk. She had just about reached her limit of endurance. It wouldn't do for him to mention that, however. Miss Independence would get her back up again. He suppressed the tug of sympathy he felt and led the way to the door of the apartment building.

An elderly woman hurried to greet them when he rang. She welcomed them in French, introduced herself as Madame Gautier and guided them to a door off the main hall.

"A moment, please. I have something for you." She went inside and returned with a basket. "A small repast, compliments of Monsieur Mercier." She glanced up the stairs, reached into the pocket of her apron and gave him a key. "Room 304. There is no lift."

Grant thanked her and handed the basket to Marie. They doggedly climbed the couple of flights of stairs which were steep and rather close.

As soon as they entered the room, Marie collapsed on the chaise longue by the window, kicked off her shoes and announced, "I have to sleep."

"How about a glass of wine?" Grant asked, noticing the neck of the bottle peeking out of the basket. Their little repast at the café had been on the light side, and he was starved. He silently thanked Mercier for providing something, anything. He would even eat escargot if that was what was in their care package.

Marie had already stretched out and closed her eyes. He shrugged, picked up the basket where she'd dropped it and fixed himself a bite of supper. Ham and cheese, a squishy pear, gooey pastry and a so-so Bordeaux composed his first Parisian meal.

He sat at the tiny little corner table and watched Marie sleep as he ate and sipped the wine. She lay on her side, one hand curled under her face. Her hair was mussed, her clothes wrinkled and her feet bare.

Band-Aids covered the small cuts on her soles. He

should check those tomorrow and make sure they were healing properly. If she would let him. Even her toes were cute. The nails were still shiny with pearly pink polish despite her ordeal.

How could anyone be more opposite than their outward appearance? She looked innocent, wide-eyed and dainty, a real lightweight in all respects. Incredibly cute in jeans and a ball cap. When dressed to the hilt, as she probably was at those embassy parties, he imagined she would qualify as glitzy, high-class arm candy any man would kill to escort. And yet, Grant now sensed a deep strength in Marie, a real core of steel, fearlessness and pure dedication. That was what attracted him most.

But she was beautiful, he thought with a smile. And sexy. Maybe she thought that was all he saw in her, but she was so wrong. Making love that soon after meeting had only reinforced her thinking that, and he knew he shouldn't have done it. Refusing her had just been beyond him.

He wondered how she saw him, and the temptation to check that out was almost overpowering. *Cheating,* his conscience warned yet again. Not fair to her to have that edge when he tried to win her over.

Nope, he decided, he would do this the right way. She had told him honestly what she considered his worst fault, and he had taken that to heart.

He had already stopped babying her. God, that was so hard to do. She made him want to wrap her up and never let anything ugly touch her ever again. The need to protect was a little too firmly ingrained in his psyche, and he had to watch that or he'd lose her for sure.

She wanted respect for her brain power and her abilities. Grant didn't imagine she had experienced much of that considering the way she looked and the pretense she'd had to employ to do her undercover work. It was high time someone showed confidence in her as an agent and as a woman. That was something unique he could offer her that she'd appreciate. Maybe she could even learn to love a man who saw the real her. That is, if he could convince her that he did.

With a last long look at her curled up so enticingly on that old fainting couch, he poured himself a second glass of wine, toasted her silently and went into the bedroom to sleep alone.

"Get up, slugabed. We have work to do," Marie ordered, shaking Grant's shoulder.

She had slept soundly, which continued to surprise her. Her old friend insomnia must have allowed Grant to take its place since he'd come into her life. Why was it that he gave her such a feeling of security, especially in view of their circumstances?

She ought to be on edge every minute considering that plus the unsettling attraction she felt for him. Didn't make sense.

And she should have gotten fully dressed before waking him. When she woke up after several hours' sleep, she had removed her wrinkled slacks and shirt and donned the knit shirt and shorts she usually slept in to finish out the night in comfort.

"What time is it?" he asked, sitting up in bed, immediately alert. He ran a hand through his hair and it spiked. That and the trace of morning beard gave him a thoroughly disreputable appearance. Now why did that make her smile?

"Seven. Sun's up." She wanted nothing more than to crawl into bed with him as she had done before. He looked so deliciously rumpled, his muscles flexing as he stretched. Her gaze landed on his chest. *Oh, man.*

She wished he didn't excite her the way he did, the way no guy ever had. She had thought she was immune to this need she had only read about before she met him.

Maybe it was because he didn't push it. All he had to do to make her want him was to *be*. She truly liked Grant, and she wanted him so fiercely she was probably attributing qualities to him that didn't even exist. Yet he really was so radically different from the only men she had known well in her life, her stepfather and her ex-fiancé.

She realized she might have on those old rose-colored glasses she had sworn she would never wear. Looking at a lover through those could prove disastrous.

Not that she loved him, of course. It was pure sexual attraction. Couldn't be more to it than that, could there? Surely not in this short a time.

His questioning smile interrupted her tumbling thoughts, almost making her dizzy.

"What?" she asked, feeling breathless.

"You might want to hop up and get out of here before I uncover." He looked down at the sheet draped just below his naval. His bare naval. Then he looked pointedly at her breasts, which were peaking beneath the T-shirt minus bra. "Unless you'd like to stay," he added, the smile widening.

"Oh." He obviously slept nude. Marie jumped up and headed for the door. "I'll…just go and…make coffee or something."

She heard his chuckle as she closed the door behind her. Oddly enough, it didn't upset her that he knew she wanted him. The fact that he hadn't taken advantage of that gave her a warm feeling inside.

He could have had her without a word, and they both knew it, but he kept his promise to her. That smacked of respect, didn't it?

Wasn't respect what she wanted most from a man? Wasn't that the most important thing? She sighed loud and long, shaking her head. Maybe it wasn't what she wanted most right at this moment, but coffee would have to suffice for now.

"That coffee smells good," Grant commented as he came out of the bedroom. He stretched and groaned. "Did you sleep okay?"

"Like a baby." Marie poured him a cup, determined to ignore the fact that they were both half-dressed. At least he had put on his shorts and shirt. No, she would not focus on how those fit. Or look at his legs. She and Grant were just two agents, intent on their mission. That's all they could be and she accepted that. Might as well be pleasant about it. Pleasant, but professional.

"Sorry I was so grumpy last night…and before, too."

He took a chair at the table and sipped the hot brew. "Well, I guess you were due. I'll bet you've been Miss Cheery Pollyanna for months on the job, haven't you?"

She laughed, relieved that he wasn't bringing up

her earlier reaction to him. "Right. And it is wearing, believe me. It's good to drop it for a while. Thanks for understanding."

"No problem. We all need a break from nice sometimes."

She sat down with her own coffee and let herself enjoy a moment of camaraderie. Good. They were playing it casual, merely friendly. This could work. "You're okay, Tyndal."

"So are you, Beauclair," he said, plucking a leftover sweet roll out of the basket he'd left there last night and offering it to her. "Any ideas how we should approach our subject?"

She bit into the roll and thought about it for a minute, then nodded. "I think I should call Bahktar when we get his number. Advise him that Shapur's unavailable and that I have what he wants. I'll persuade him to meet with me to hand it over. Then I'll see if I can find out where they stashed Cynthia. If he knows."

Marie licked her finger and waited for his response. His jaw tightened. His eyebrows rose as he broke eye contact and shifted in his chair. She'd bet he was about to explode with a protest and was ready for it.

But he said nothing. Instead, he got up, took his cell phone out of his pocket and made a call.

Marie listened as he spoke a few words to Mercier. Not a word about her, surprisingly. Mostly he just listened while Mercier did the talking. Grant clicked the phone shut, put it away and looked her dead in the eye. "Okay, we have Bahktar's cell number, the one Shapur called from the clinic."

She finished her coffee. "I'll get ready, then make the call."

It was too early in the day, but she didn't want to give Grant a lot of time to think about it or he might change his mind about going along with her plan.

"Remember, it will have to be somewhere with lots of people around," he said. His lips firmed and he shook his head. He paced for a minute, then stopped and looked at her. "Are you sure you want to do this, Marie? I have a feeling this guy is not one we want to monkey around with."

"Sit for a minute." She motioned him back to his chair, hoping he'd calm down, stay reasonable and listen. "Look, I've thought it out," she told him. "A stranger calling him, one who knows he's involved in this, won't go down well in any case. If it's a woman, he won't like it, but he's not as likely to run."

"Why do you think that?"

"Well, females probably rate very low in his estimation, hardly worth thinking about unless they have something he wants. Considering this plan of his, he must not like them much in the first place."

"Yeah." Grant huffed with disgust. "And considering the culture that spawned him, he probably thinks you're all subhuman."

"Right," Marie agreed. "So it will never enter his mind that I'm an agent. If he knows I have the number he needs, he'll see me. And if I play it right, he might give us a clue where Cynthia is being held."

"As you said, *if* he knows," Grant qualified. "It's possible he left all those details up to Shapur and the goons the doctor hired. Why would Shapur have told him where she was?"

Marie shook her head. "I don't know. Maybe he didn't, but we have to try to find out, don't we? That's the whole justification for the meeting instead of going at him like a SWAT team."

Grant shrugged. "It is a long shot, but yes, we do have to try. Your plan makes sense."

And that final admission had cost him dearly, she could tell. She slowly released a breath of relief. Grant wasn't going to contradict her plan. He actually trusted her to handle Bahktar.

"Did Mercier find out anything about him that I should know going in?"

Grant reached across the table and took her hand as he began to speak. "He has an import/export business here in Paris. He presents himself as an expatriate but has made regular and frequent trips back to Iran over the last fifteen years. He has no family that could be identified, either here or there. The wealth he has amassed is tied up in his business assets. Not liquid, apparently."

Marie nodded. "That explains his motive for seeking ransoms. Why involve Shapur?"

"An easy mark for extortion. Shapur was loosely affiliated with the shah. We suspect Bahktar might originally have been positioned here to keep tabs on the royal family in exile. Intelligence reports now connect him to several arms dealers, probably his main source of income. No surprise there. He's gathering capital for the next buy."

"No wife or lady friend? Is he gay?"

"He's had female companions, all temporary. No males. Of course, that carries a death sentence in his country, so he wouldn't be open about it." Grant held her gaze. "But if you're planning to entice information out of him with your feminine wiles, I really wouldn't advise it."

Marie smiled and squeezed his fingers. "And I wouldn't try it. One dangerous man in my life at a time, a hard-and-fast rule."

"Am I, Marie? In your life?"

"You're my partner, aren't you? Right now, that has to be enough. Is it?"

His expression revealed nothing. "I told you. Whatever you want."

Marie disengaged her hand and got up from the table. She couldn't look at him as she replied. "What I want is trust, Grant. You are trusting me with the lead on this and that's a start."

"If you require trust, then you ought to give it. Do you trust me, Marie?"

She did look at him then, searching those serious blue-gray eyes. "I trust you with my life."

He got up and started toward her. She raised a hand before he got within reach, and he stopped, waiting, watching her, saying more with those expressive eyes than words could have done.

Marie meant what she had said; she did trust him. However, she could see what looked very much like love in those mesmerizing eyes, and it wasn't something she was ready to acknowledge. She could too easily return it, and then where would she be?

But what if she never saw him again after today? One way or another, this meeting with Bahktar would end this mission. It would be over. They would be over.

Unless she accepted a place within COMPASS, she doubted that she and Grant would ever meet again. She would have to refuse the job offer or get caught up in an affair that could only end with one of them losing his or her position.

But if she had no intention of ever seeing him again, why deny herself? Or him, for that matter? Why not have one more splendid memory of perfect lovemaking? He was the best, no doubt about that. She would never find another man like him.

Maybe, just maybe, that satisfaction would make it easier for both of them to let go. Sort of like a private, final goodbye…kiss.

"Grant?" she asked tentatively.

"Yes?" His gaze held hers.

"It's early yet." She held out her arms.

He gave her a smile that would melt the coldest heart and came to her. There were no questions, no avowals, no words at all. His kiss drowned all her doubts; he obviously had none in the first place.

Marie clung to him as he carried her back to the bed where he'd slept. She imagined it still warm from his body as he lay down with her.

His hands explored every inch of her as they peeled away the loose shirt and shorts slowly. He moved as if they had all the time in the world and nothing else to do.

She trailed kisses along his neck, loving the taste of his skin, inhaling the subtle scent of his aftershave and feeling the smoothness of muscle against her lips. He overwhelmed her senses and filled them with pleasure, swept her up in a wave of need that kept rising without breaking.

He uttered wordless sounds of encouragement as he stroked and touched and enticed. Memories of their last time spurred her to hurry him on, but he would not give in.

For what seemed hours, he drew her closer and closer to that moment when he would take her, claim her and join her in the surrender of power that left both of them breathless.

Could she let go again, knowing how it had left her so vulnerable before? But she wanted so desperately, so keenly, there was no going back, no saying no. She wanted it, and she wanted *him* more than anything else in her world. This one last time, she would know how it felt to belong.

"Be with me," he whispered against her ear as he entered her finally, fully, and began to move.

For once in her life, Marie gave herself, openly, honestly and without reservation. It was like dying. Like being reborn. Like loving. She cried out and held him with all her strength, wishing to the depths of her soul that she never had to let go.

For the longest time, neither of them said anything, but eventually breath and reason returned.

"Are you all right?" Grant asked.

"No," she admitted, sniffing, not even caring how she sounded. Her world was upside down. "But, please…"

"I know. Be quiet," he crooned, smoothing her tangled

hair and laying a kiss on top of her head. "Sleep a little now. There's plenty of time and I'll watch the clock."

His voice soothed her, took away the need to think, and she slept.

Mamud Bahktar closed his phone and frowned in thought. Shapur had hired a woman? Small wonder he had not shared the names of the kidnappers he contracted. This one had been in charge of luring the young women out of their safety zones so they could be taken, or so she said. Brazen female. Demanding to meet in a public place signaled she was no idiot. Perhaps she guessed he would want to kill her.

She had said Shapur and his men were dead, killed in a gas explosion at the clinic where the doctor lived. Perhaps it was just as well, since he had planned to get rid of Shapur after one more abduction anyway.

The numbered account would contain enough to begin the arms transaction when added to what he'd be able to borrow against his assets. In any event, he would have to meet with the woman to get that number.

He didn't like women involved in business, especially *his* business, but he might be able to use her for one last abduction, provided she had male associates who would do the actual deed.

Mamud took out the photo he carried of his betrothed and looked at it for inspiration. A worthy one she was, too. Young, dark-eyed innocence.

He glanced at the other picture that he had tucked away behind hers. So different yet with the same aura of youth and vulnerability. This one was smiling openly, unaware she was being captured on film, a delicate little blonde about to drive away in her very expensive, bright red convertible. A rich mark. The one who got away.

He really had to do something about finding her.

Chapter 17

Marie couldn't believe Grant had left the bed without a word. He'd been gone when she woke up, and now she heard him on the phone in the other room.

She pulled on her shorts and shirt, almost afraid to face him because she wasn't sure how she would react. They had a job to do, however, and no time to waste. When she joined him, he ended his conversation and held out the phone to her. "Whenever you're ready. Mercier will have our backup available within the hour, but they'll hold off until we give the word. I was just about to wake you."

Marie had made the call and arranged the meeting, though Bahktar had insisted on choosing the locale. What he suggested had sounded perfect and should be teeming with people, so she didn't object.

Then she quickly excused herself to grab a shower and dress for the meeting with Bahktar.

Grant was pacing when she returned to the room. She wore all black—her wrinkle-proof pants, a long-sleeved, body-hugging jersey and a crocheted beret covering most of her hair. The shoes were black flats. "Well?" she asked as she joined him.

His gaze traveled over her slowly. "You look like a baby terrorist. All you need is an AK-47."

"Bring one along if you can get it," she replied with a twist of her lips. "He ordered me to come unarmed and to dress so he would know I wasn't carrying without having to frisk me."

"I don't see any place you could hide one."

She gave a little tilt of her head, lifted one foot and pulled up her pant leg to show her little Glock 27 taped above her ankle. The weapon was used for backup by some agents but was perfect for her primarily since her hands were small. Grant nodded his approval.

In spite of that, she could see that he was itching to call the whole thing off. It showed in every shift of his body, in the tick of his jaw, the worry crinkle between his eyebrows.

Marie hated to see him so worried, but at least she knew that it wasn't because he thought she was incapable. He just cared about her. Maybe loved her. *Did* love her, she admitted.

"I'll be okay," she said, faking a smile. She could admit to herself that she was apprehensive, but she'd never let him see that. This was her chance to do what she had been trained to do.

Grant nodded again. "You know I'll be close by. One wrong move on his part, and I'm taking him out."

Marie couldn't and didn't argue with the wisdom of that. There might not be time to reach for her own weapon if Bahktar decided she was expendable. Somehow, she didn't think he would risk violence in the crowd of tourists that would be hanging around. "Why'd he choose Place de la Concorde, I wonder?"

Grant checked his weapon as he answered. "The obelisk. That's where the guillotine was located. A place of execution. Ready to back out now?"

"No. I don't think he'll make a move there. He might try to follow me to a more opportune spot, though. You'll watch for that."

"Like a hawk."

Marie watched as he struggled with the need to dissuade her from doing this. She saw the moment he lost the fight.

"Look, let me do it, Marie. I'll tell him you hired me to meet with him in your place. You can watch my back."

"Not gonna happen, Grant. We go in as planned. I'll chat him up a little, see what I can get on Rivers's location in exchange for the number. He'll believe I don't know where she is, since Shapur and the others were killed unexpectedly and never told me where they had her. I'll promise him her ransom if I can deliver her alive."

"He won't trust you to do it. And he won't care if she's alive or not. Maybe he won't care enough about the money if it means letting you go when you can identify him as part of it."

"I'm doing this, Grant. If he looks at me cross-eyed, shoot him, but let me get a few questions in first, okay?"

He blew out a sharp breath and shook his head. "All right, all right. But be extremely careful, you hear?"

"I hear." She glanced at the cheap watch she had picked up in Amsterdam. "It's time we left if I'm going to beat him there."

She felt jazzed, up for it, confident things would work out. A positive attitude worked wonders.

Grant grabbed her by the shoulders and kissed her soundly on the mouth. She hardly had time to react before he released her.

"I love you, Marie. I know you don't want to hear that or deal with it now, but I need you to know."

"I know," she said, and would have said more, but he shook her gently, interrupting.

"Don't you get yourself killed, Marie! Or even hurt. I mean it, don't do *anything* risky." He cradled her head with one hand, her body with the other and held her tight. "Promise me."

Ear pressed to his chest, she could hear his heart beating ninety to nothing. Or maybe it was her own pulse racing. For a long time he held her fast, as if he'd never release her. She didn't even think of pulling away. It felt so good to have someone who cared this much. When had she ever felt anything like this?

When he did let her go, she touched her fingers to her lips and a smile welled up behind them. He was so damn sincere. He *loved* her.

He had seen her at her very worst, bedraggled, grouchy, complaining, bossy, weepy. Never seen her at her best. She hadn't had a chance yet to show him her good side. Maybe that was mostly manufactured anyway.

Did she even have a good side? She wasn't quite sure who she really was when not pressed to play a role, because she had been doing it for so long.

Still, he *loved* her.

Never in her life had she felt any closer to anyone. Not her parents, not her friends and certainly not her coworkers. Maybe she loved him, too, though she didn't have a very good handle on the love thing. Certainly no comparables. The sex was great, but there was much more to how she felt about Grant than merely the physical.

He was so open, accepting and truly thoughtful, even if that thoughtfulness was often a little overbearing. She understood why and she understood him.

What they were about to do went against every grain of instinct he possessed, letting her put herself out front this way. Also, this was probably the only time in his life he had ever taken the backseat on an op. That couldn't be easy.

"I promise. No heroics," she told him. And she meant it at the time. She even kissed him back to seal the deal.

The sky was gray, heavy with clouds when they left the apartment. Traffic was heavy, too. It was nearly ten o'clock, and the meeting was set for ten thirty.

Grant drove down the Champs-Elysées to where the Tuileries Gardens began, whipped down a side street and left the car there. They walked side by side in the mist, silent, each getting psyched up for the meeting.

He stopped her before they turned the corner onto the main thoroughfare. "Remember your promise," he said with a featherlight touch to her cheek. Concern clouded his eyes and put that deep little dent between his eyebrows.

She smoothed it out with her fingertip and grinned up at him. "I'll be *fine*. Just stay close by. If I need you to jump in, I'll do this." She opened her left hand and placed it over her upper chest, her fingers splayed.

He nodded, placed his hand over hers and gave it a pat.

Marie strolled along well ahead of him as if she had nothing better to do than kill time. She wandered around the equestrian statue that marked the intersection of the East-West and North-South approaches. The obelisk stood in the midst of a large oval area with fountains at either end. The area was much bigger than it had looked in photos.

The mist turned to definite sprinkles. Then it began to rain. Thank goodness it wasn't a downpour, but it was heavy enough to thin out the tourists who were now dashing for cover. They were her protection, and they were disappearing, unaware of how she might need them.

She walked on to the nearest fountain, glancing now and then at the area around the obelisk for a man in a suit with a red tie. That had been his idea. She had told him she would wear all black, which really was about all she had with her anyway.

Place de la Concorde spooked her a little. During the revolution nearly three thousand people had had their heads chopped on that spot where the obelisk stood now. Locals declared then that cattle wouldn't even approach the place because the smell of blood was so strong. She imagined she could smell it now over two centuries later.

She hoped Bahktar's choice of rendezvous didn't have a hidden meaning.

There he was now, approaching. He looked around fifty, rather handsome, tall, dark, neat mustache and stylishly cropped hair. He was wearing an expensive, tailor-made raincoat. The picture of a well-to-do businessman, impatient to complete his transaction and get somewhere out of the rain. The knot and upper half of his red tie stood out against the white shirt and gray lapels. He carried his closed umbrella like a cane.

Marie wandered to the edge of the fountain, where rain was disturbing the surface. Out of the corner of her eye, she watched Grant pass by her and head toward the obelisk. He paused near it, ignoring Bahktar, and took out what appeared to be a guidebook. His glance went from book to monument and back again as if comparing written facts with reality.

He was wearing her baseball cap. In his loose, all-weather jacket, worn jeans and scuffed running shoes, Grant looked and moved like a determined tourist with limited time to see the sights.

Bahktar watched him closely for a few minutes, then shrugged with flagging interest when Grant headed in the direction of one of the statues, still paging through the little book. Where had he secured that prop? It was probably the car manual, she realized.

She waited a few moments, took a deep breath and began her approach, fingers tucked into the flat pockets on the front of her slacks. She kept her head down, watching the uneven pavers and the gathering puddles at her feet. She was nearly soaked through but hardly noticed that discomfort.

Bravado spurred her on, right up to the wrought iron fence that surrounded the obelisk. She stood about six feet from Bahktar and sensed him staring at her profile.

"You want the last installment transferred to the account?" she asked without preamble. She spoke in English using a Flemish accent. "There is a price."

Bahktar walked closer to her. Marie kept her eyes averted, waiting to see how he would respond.

"You have the ransom?" he asked, his words clipped but sounding quite relaxed considering the tense situation.

"Not yet. Shapur had the girl stashed somewhere, and I couldn't find her. If you know where, tell me and I'll handle the switch. If you don't, our business here is finished."

"Not quite. I believe you have a number for me."

"First the girl's location. If you don't want her ransom, I do. That's the price of your precious number. I would have used it myself, but he didn't give me the name of the bank. You have that, I presume?"

"Give me the number or I will kill you," he said succinctly. "I will kill you right here."

And he might try that, Marie thought. Almost all of the foot traffic in the area had disappeared. Except for Grant. She couldn't see him without turning around, but trusted he was within range.

"Kill me and forgo the stash Shapur sacked away for you? I don't think so." She looked straight at him then, chin up, and she smiled with confidence, running the bluff for all she was worth.

And saw instant shock and recognition in his eyes. *Omigod*, he *knew* who she was! How did he know?

She immediately placed her open left hand on her chest, the signal to Grant for help. With her right arm straight down, she lifted her leg behind her and went for the gun near her ankle, hoping Bahktar wouldn't notice what she was doing until she had it in hand.

He moved like lightning, caught her off balance and grabbed her in a stranglehold, his back against the fence. One arm clamped her to him; the other braced her shoulder, his knife at her neck.

"Let her go!" Grant demanded, his Glock leveled at Bahktar. And also at her, since she was his shield. She felt the blade. Where the devil had that come from, the umbrella? He must have planned all along to dispense with her silently right here by the obelisk.

"Drop the pistol," Bahktar said to Grant with deadly calm. "If you do not, I will slice her jugular. Do it *now.*"

Marie had to do something. Grant would probably concede in an attempt to save her, but she knew she was done for, no matter what he did, unless she got out of Bahktar's grasp.

"He won't shoot you without an order," she gasped, addressing her captor. "Loosen up and I'll call him off. Kill me and it's over for you. I hired him for protection. He's a pro."

She felt the pressure lighten a little, but the knife still lay too close to the carotid for her to make a move. "Back off!" she called to Grant. "It's okay. I've got it covered."

Grant still stood about twenty feet away, his weapon out of reach. He looked ready to pounce. She knew he had a backup under his jacket and dearly hoped he was ready to use it. She made the sign of a pistol with her hand.

"It's on the paper in my left pocket," she replied easily. "Get it yourself."

He let go of her waist with his left arm and slid his fingers into the tight flat pocket. As she'd hoped, his right arm shifted, creating a wider gap between her neck and the knife.

Marie grasped his right wrist, kicked backward to his knee and quickly threw him to the ground. He slashed out wildly as he fell, slicing her leg with a vicious swipe of the blade.

A shot rang out and Bahktar lay still. She ripped the gun off her leg and released the safety. The wound near where she'd had it taped began to throb and she felt faint. She sat down on the pavers to check the damage.

"Lie back," Grant ordered as he ran to her. He knelt and pushed on her shoulder. "Dammit, Marie!" He had his belt off and was wrapping it around her thigh as a tourniquet.

She groaned and blinked to clear the rainwater from her eyes. And saw Bahktar sit up, knife in hand and start to lunge.

Grant! Without thinking, she put a bullet right in the middle of Bahktar's forehead. He dropped like a rock.

"Oh, God, I…killed him!"

Now they would never find Cynthia Rivers. She had failed her mission.

That was her last thought before she fainted.

Chapter 18

"The next plane, Tyndal," Mercier ordered. "Be on it."

"I'm not leaving her. Fire me if you have to, but I'm here until she's on her feet and I know she's okay."

A moment's silence ensued. Grant tried to steady his breathing and sound reasonable, not the basket case he had been in the hours since Marie had been admitted to the hospital.

"Look, sir, I just need another day or so before I report. I've given you all the details, and everything's square with the local authorities. I can't just abandon Marie here in Paris. Let me wait until she's released from the hospital and I'll bring her with me when I come back."

"She's not coming," Mercier informed him. "I just spoke with her. Grant, don't make this harder for her, okay?"

"What do you mean?" Grant asked, a chill suffusing his body.

"Give her some space," Mercier suggested. "If you don't, we'll lose her."

And if he did, *he* might lose her, Grant thought.

"The decision must be *hers*. Trust me on this."

"What did she say?" Grant asked without much hope Mercier would tell him.

"She's been through a lot in a very short length of time. You can't expect her to make any life-altering decisions at this juncture. Surely you can see that. So, go tell her about Rivers, say a quick goodbye, wish her luck and get your ass back here before I send someone to get you."

Well, that was not much in the way of minced words. Grant had to admit it made sense to do as ordered, especially after Marie had accused him of hovering.

He'd done his utmost to stop doing that. Hadn't he let her walk right into that meeting with Bahktar with nothing but a peashooter and a smile to defend herself? Look how that had turned out.

What the hell did she expect now? That he'd just walk away and hope she came to her senses and saw that no man could ever love her like he did? He had already told her, shown her and done all he could to convince her.

Mercier had already hung up, assuming he'd get what he wanted with that threat. Well, maybe he would. The man had a point, even if Grant didn't like what he heard.

Okay, then. If breathing room was what Marie needed, that's what he'd give her. Up to a point, of course. If he hadn't heard from her in a week, he was coming back after her. Maybe two weeks would be better if he could stand being without her that long.

He drew in and released a fortifying breath, stuck his phone in his pocket and marched back to the elevator. She had passed out from losing so much blood and he had talked with her only once since she woke up in the hospital. All of that conversation had been about her wound before the nurse made him leave the room.

Marie would have a scar about four inches long, but she hadn't seemed the least bit upset by it. "My first badge of battle," she had said, sounding a little too proud of herself. Grant had wanted to cry, imagining that beautiful, perfect leg marred in that way.

He entered her room with a smile pasted on that didn't even reach his teeth. "How're you doing now that the goof shot's wearing off?"

"Fine! Hardly hurts at all," she replied. The perky little cheerleader ruled and Grant couldn't stand it. He knew she must feel like hell.

"They found Rivers," he told her, wanting to make her cheer for real.

"Seriously? Great! Where was she all that time?"

"Root cellar not far from the clinic's kitchen. Eric Vinland, one of our agents, managed to mind link with her and found out she was in an underground structure. The entrance was concealed by debris, so they hadn't found her until he did that."

"So, she's alive?" Marie asked, her eyes wide with hope.

"And mad as hell, they say. Dehydrated and dirty, but alive and kicking."

"Thank God. I've been so afraid I'd sealed her doom by shooting Bahktar. He is dead, right?"

"As the proverbial doorknob. You'll have to get some counseling on that, I expect."

"I know. Right now I don't feel a bit of guilt. It was him or you."

"You saved my life. Did I say thanks?"

"Not necessary. You saved me from that explosion. We're even, I guess."

Grant watched her toy with the edge of the sheet as she spoke. Was she uncomfortable with his being here? Did she think he would demand more of her than she was ready to give? Yeah, there was that little hesitant quiver of her lips. She probably wanted to say something but didn't know how without hurting his feelings.

He bit the bullet. "Mercier's ordered me home to make paperwork and get grilled. When are you being released?" *Please, please say you'll come with me,* he chanted in his mind.

"Tomorrow. They're sending someone from the embassy to escort me back to Germany. Lots to do there, clearing things up."

Grant held back the questions. Would she go back to her job there? Would she be satisfied with minor snooping after she'd tasted real action? Would she forget him the minute he was gone?

Instead of all the questions, he walked over to her bedside, took her hand, kissed her on the forehead and faked a grin. "If you get bored, come to McLean. I'll marry you and give you pretty babies to keep you busy."

She laughed and squeezed his hand. "That sounds…really interesting, Tyndal, but I'm not quite ready for that much excitement." Her gaze dropped away. "There are things I need to do before I settle anywhere. I hope you understand?"

He released her before he broke down, begged and vowed he was serious about the offer he'd made. "All right, then, but just so you know, the invitation's open-ended."

"You're leaving now?" she asked, sounding a little breathless, something, he had learned, she did when she was feeling nervous or apprehensive.

"Next plane out." He looked pointedly at his watch. "Goodbye kiss okay?"

"Goodbye kiss mandatory," she replied, and raised her face as he lowered his.

He made it a sweet one, devoid of the passion he wanted to show. Marie was a miracle that had happened to him when he had given up on miracles. Magic all over. Her lips were so soft and giving, trembling a little under his. She was the one who drew away.

How could she let it go so easily, all that they could be together? *Know that I love you with everything I am,* he thought, wishing to God he had Vinland's telepathy as a gift, that the thought would transfer.

Without another word, he gave her a last, longing look. Then he turned and left her lying there. It was the hardest goodbye ever.

The worst part was that he knew now he couldn't come back for her. The next move, if there ever was one, would have to be hers.

Grant's flight home proved uneventful, but when he deplaned and retrieved his bag, there was a surprise in the baggage area. Mercier stood there, waiting for him.

"Toss the weapon and take a walk," Bahktar added.

Marie watched Grant hesitate. He shot her a questioning look. She smiled and gave him a thumbs-up. After a few more seconds, he crouched down and laid his gun on the pavers. Slowly he backed away from it. Now there was trust, she thought, wondering if she could live up to it.

Bahktar still held her but lowered the knife a few inches. "Who are you, woman?" he asked.

Marie issued a nervous chuckle. "I'm Beauclair. Shapur hired Onders to snatch me from the embassy. Since my family wouldn't give a worthless franc for my life or anyone else's, I persuaded him to let me in on the deal and I would help him with the next mark."

"He was a fool. How did you *persuade* him?"

"Exactly how you think I did. Yeah, that, plus I promised to make it child's play to grab the next one if he'd give me 10 percent of his take."

"Shapur agreed to this?"

"We didn't tell *him*. The only time I spoke to Shapur was when he was dying after the explosion. He begged me to bring you the number and plead with you for his daughter's life."

Bahktar scoffed. "She's been dead for two years."

Marie scoffed right back. "Like I care? Let me go, I'll give you the number and you tell me where that last girl's being kept, the one from Amsterdam that Shapur's other man took. I'll do the deal and we'll split the ransom. Better deal quickly before some yahoo calls the gendarmes!"

"First the number," he insisted.

"Welcome back."

"What's up?" Grant knew it must be something big. The boss wouldn't have driven all the way out to Dulles to meet one of his agents otherwise.

Mercier shrugged. "Not much at the moment. Pretty quiet, just the way we like it. I probably jinxed us by saying that." He headed for the exit. "When we get to the office, I'll be debriefing you about the op, but on the drive back I thought we might dispense with the personal problem and get that out of the way."

"You mean Agent Beauclair." It wasn't a question. "Not a problem. I did as you suggested." Ordered, really.

Mercier shot him a thoughtful glance and continued walking. By the time they reached the parking lot and got into the car, Grant had tamped down his resentment to a manageable level. No use holding Mercier responsible for the loss of Marie.

"Good job, by the way," Mercier said as he backed out of the parking spot and began the trip back to McLean.

"That's a laugh. Marie rescued herself, basically. And I wasn't able to do a thing to save Cynthia Rivers. Thank God Vinland was able to."

Grant flashed back to the confrontation at the obelisk in Place de la Concorde. "Marie was severely injured because of me. She might have been killed."

"She told me you played it exactly right, followed her signs to the letter. You both took Bahktar out. That's what is important, Grant. The kidnapping spree is over and it wouldn't be if you hadn't been there."

"Is this the debriefing already?"

Mercier smiled. "No. This is the little talk where I commend you for teamwork, reluctant as you were. You've been a loner in the past, but you aren't one by nature, I think."

"I work better by myself."

"Sometimes that's true but sometimes not. Delegation and trust are the main things you need to work on. You led the investigation to Holland, then on to Paris with your expertise. Otherwise it would have been a dead end in Germany. Eric Vinland used an ability you don't have to locate Rivers. That was his part of the job, and he did it well. Marie employed her CIA training to the max, both in her escape and in every other instance. Give her that credit, Grant. You don't have to do everything all by yourself. It's a lesson it took me a while to learn, too."

"I lost objectivity."

Mercier nodded. "It happens when you're personally involved with a partner. I know from experience. That's why I discourage it whenever I can."

Grant said nothing. He couldn't pry into the boss's life, but he did wonder.

"I met Solange on an op a few years ago, shortly after we organized SEXTANT. Fell like a damn bungee jumper. Nearly cost both her life and mine."

"That's why you ordered me to cut Marie loose."

"No, I didn't order that. I said to give her some space to make up her own mind."

Grant's resentment returned with the force of a blow to the head. "I've lost her because I followed orders."

Mercier shook his head. "No. If you lost her, it's because you held on too tight, rushed her, tried to think for her and do for her. She probably resented that. Wouldn't you? Anyway, you don't want a woman who doesn't want you back, do you?"

Yes, by God, he did. He wanted her any way he could have her, but it was too late now. "Look, I already have a mother, okay? Could we drop this before I say more than I ought to?"

"All right. But if you need to talk about it later, we can. We're a team, Grant, and all of us in SEXTANT and COMPASS are here for you, whether the issue is personal or professional. Ours is a tight group. Sometimes discussing things with people on the outside is hard because of the security aspect. We depend on each other."

"Fine. I get it. No heart-to-hearts with Mom."

"Oh, absolutely have those. Mothers thrive on soothing their wounded cubs. How are your parents, by the way?" Mercier asked.

"I didn't contact them while I was on assignment. I'll call when I get back to my apartment."

"Call now," Mercier suggested. "They're probably worried."

Grant dutifully took out his cell phone to make the call. He might as well get used to Mercier's dogged interference.

His mother would sense his mood the minute he spoke to her. She would question him about it, too, but he couldn't tell her about his losing Marie and make her worry.

Had he always protected her automatically from any problem he'd encountered? And Dad expected a stiff upper lip. Old army, that was Dad. Handle it yourself. *Be strong for everybody. Be responsible.*

Maybe he had gone a little too far with that.

His mother answered on the first ring.

"Hey, Mom. How's it going? I thought I'd let you know I'm back in one piece and everything's cool."

She picked up on his tone immediately as he feared she would.

"Yeah, I'm doing all right," he insisted, but her questions were rapid-fire and to the point. For the first time he really took note of how incredibly strong she sounded, strong and capable of handling more than he had ever imagined.

Grant shot a glance at Mercier's profile and saw his subtle smile. A dare? What the hell. "I met somebody and it didn't work out. That's all. Yes, Mom, she was really important to me, and I'm a wreck right now."

She didn't fall apart, weep all over the phone and dissolve into hysterics. Instead, she launched into all the staunch, motherly platitudes designed to salve his pride and let him know he was the center of her universe.

Yeah, he'd had it wrong all along where she was concerned. Five minutes later he closed the phone and put it away. "She's sending me a cake. My favorite. And I expect she'll show up by the end of the week to console me with chicken soup. I feel like a wimp."

Mercier laughed out loud. "No, no, you're making real progress! Showing your *sensitive* side."

"Yeah, right. Too little, too late," Grant muttered. It would take a lot more than cake, soup and Mom's reassurance about all those other fish in the sea to help him get over Marie.

Chapter 19

Marie found Grant's apartment easily enough. Mercier had actually encouraged her to go there and gave her directions.

The three weeks she had spent without Grant had firmly reinforced the decision she'd made the last time they had made love. She had wanted to be certain and needed the alone time to ask herself some hard questions about her life and form some answers.

The first dealt with her mother and stepfather. Somehow, some way, she decided she had to forgive them for her own peace of mind.

She investigated and found that Barry, her stepfather, had been confined to a nursing home for almost fifteen years, paralyzed from a shooting. At least he hadn't done any damage to any other little girls.

No charges were filed, but Marie had to wonder who had shot him. She did discover that her mother had taken a job at a pistol and pawn shop out in Decatur a week before it had happened. Maybe her mom had learned the truth. Marie dropped the inquiries then and there. It simply didn't matter anymore. Those bridges were burned, but she forgave.

Her fiancé, Thomas, had married. Then divorced. Then married and divorced again. Poor Tom couldn't seem to get it right. It wouldn't do a bit of good to wish him well, but she did anyway.

All that remained was the necessity of eliminating what she could of Grant's angst. Hence the visit today. During the effort to make it happen, she had come to understand Grant's compulsion to make things right for her, to do everything possible to save her grief and hurt, even when she resented it, didn't appreciate it and misread his motive. He'd already forgiven all that. He loved her.

She winked at her companion as she rang Grant's doorbell and waited.

He wore a look of shock when he opened the door and saw her. "Hi. What are you... I thought you weren't coming back."

She raised her hands in a here-I-am gesture, then brought them together on his beard-rough cheeks and gave him a kiss hello. "Hey, Tyndal. What's up?"

He responded as if she was his last breath and he couldn't wait to take it. To take *her*. When he grabbed and kissed her, Marie forgot about why she had come, how she had gotten there and all she'd planned to say.

Greedy for all she had missed, she threw herself into

the kiss and stopped only when the sound of girlish laughter interrupted.

She pushed at Grant's chest and stood back, still grasping his forearms. "Wait, *wait!* I brought some-one to see you," she gasped, trying to catch her breath and steady it.

He finally noticed the woman standing beside her. His look was questioning.

Marie cleared her throat and gestured to the guest. "Elizabeth Karg. She lives in New York. Albany."

Still obviously confused, he held out a hand. "Ms. Karg?"

The woman laughed merrily as she took it in both of hers. "Don't you know me, Grant?"

He squinted and peered at her more closely, then his mouth dropped open. He exhaled the name. "Betty? Betty Schonrock?"

"Well, I *was,* once upon a time. I came to apologize for shaking you up so much all those years ago. Marie told me how you've worried about me ever since, and I wanted to come by and thank you for all that concern. I really am sorry for that, but as you can see, I'm per-fectly fine. Married. Four kids. Great husband." She patted his hand. "You can stop worrying now."

Grant took a step back, shaking his head in disbelief. "I see. Well, uh, will you come in? I could…make coffee or something." He looked at Marie, a dawning look of wonder on his face.

"Oh, I can't stay," Betty said, laughing at his expres-sion. "My family came with me, and they're waiting to do a little sightseeing. I promised I wouldn't be long.

It is so nice to see you again, though." She shook her head. "You sure have changed! I guess I have, too. For the better, I promise. Maybe not better physically."

"You're *beautiful*, Betty. Absolutely beautiful. You always were."

"Thanks!" She turned to Marie and winked. "He always was a sweetie. Take care now, and if you two are ever up in Albany, please stop by to see us. Marie has the address."

He couldn't seem to let go of Betty's hand. "But where did you go?" he asked. "And why?"

She frowned. "Family troubles no one wants to talk about, especially me. Werner helped me disappear until my parents left for the States. Then we got married and spent a few years in the country near Stuttgart with his folks. Marie will tell you all about it now that you've seen for yourself I'm not dead and gone."

"You survived," Grant said. "I can't get over it!"

"I do appreciate that you kept on trying to find me when everyone else gave up. Good thing you didn't succeed, I guess, but it's really touching that you tried."

The two shared a long moment's wordless reunion as Marie looked on.

Then Betty gave a nod and broke the spell. "I'll just leave you and Marie alone now and wish you the very best. Maybe we'll see each other again sometime."

She clutched Marie's hand in farewell. "Thanks for arranging this, Marie, and for offering to finance the trip. It was so nice to meet you and to see you again, Grant. Goodbye for now." She gave him another hug, then reached up and pinched his cheek. "You sure filled out nicely, beanpole!"

With that, she was gone again.

Marie smiled at Grant's awestruck expression. "She's a doll. I can see why you had such a crush on her. Uh, it *is* over now, isn't it? She's taken." Marie snapped her fingers in front of his face. "Grant?"

He shook off the shock and reached for her, enfolding her again in those big, strong arms that felt like heaven after too many weeks apart. "You are amazing, Beauclair, you know that? How did you ever *find* her?"

"When you said you couldn't figure why she left when she had everything going for her, I wondered if it might not have been abuse at home."

"Same reason you and your family parted company," Grant said. He shook his head. "But I looked so hard for her. It was as if she had dropped off the planet."

"Yes. Well, I have more resources to find people than you did then. I had some downtime while I was winding things up on the case I'd been working. Since I was in Germany already and you had me wondering about her, too, I kept digging until I found her."

"I'm amazed that you'd do something fantastic like this, just for me. What can I say?"

"How about *thanks and let's play catch up?* It has been a long time since Paris."

"So it has, and here you've found me a wreck, all scuzzy looking and needing a shave and a shower."

"A shower sounds great. Have you got two towels?"

He hugged her again, nearly crushing her. "Thank God you came. Promise you'll stay?"

"Guess I'll have to. I'm on the payroll as the new

liaison between COMPASS and the Company. We'll be coordinating a lot, I expect. Can you stand it?"

Grant leaned his head back to look down at her, his hands still gripping her waist. "I meant stay *here*. With me."

She looked around the typical bachelor digs, littered with books, clothes and newspapers. Two beer cans lay crushed on his coffee table, a monstrosity he'd probably picked up at a yard sale. The lumpy sofa looked clean, but that was its only saving grace. "Where else would I go? This is such a neat place you've got here. Real homey."

He looked around and winced. "You mean, *homely,* don't you? We'll junk everything and redecorate immediately. Anything you want, we'll do it."

"Anything?" She grinned. "Okay, let's tackle the bedroom first, then. I have some great ideas for in there."

"You haven't even seen it yet," he said, taking her hand to lead her there.

"Well, I wasn't talking about replacing the drapes." She pinched his arm playfully. "Your original offer still good? You know, that marriage and babies deal?"

His grin widened. "Absolutely. The loner thing was getting really old."

"For me, too. We'll make a good team, don't you think?"

"The best. I can be a real team player now that you showed me how. And I don't hover anymore." He shook his head. "Never hover."

"Yeah, well, we'll see how you do. Promise you'll let me make at least half the decisions?"

He nodded with enthusiasm. "Beginning right now. Shower or sex? Your choice."

She laughed. "What a wealth of options! Did I tell you I love you yet?"

"Oh, yeah, you did," he assured her seriously. "You said it very well, but I'd still like to hear the actual words."

"Every day I'll say it, in every way I know how," she promised and uttered the phrase she had never said before to anyone. "I love you."

* * * * *

*Celebrate 60 years of pure reading
pleasure with Harlequin®!*
*Silhouette® Romantic Suspense is celebrating with
the glamour-filled, adrenaline-charged series*
LOVE IN 60 SECONDS
*starting in April 2009.
Six stories that promise to bring the
glitz of Las Vegas, the danger of revenge,
the mystery of a missing diamond, family scandals
and ripped-from-the-headlines intrigue.
Get your heart racing as love happens
in sixty seconds!*

Enjoy a sneak peek of
USA TODAY *bestselling author
Marie Ferrarella's*
*THE HEIRESS'S 2-WEEK AFFAIR
Available April 2009 from
Silhouette® Romantic Suspense.*

Eight years ago Matt Shaffer had vanished out of Natalie Rothchild's life, leaving behind a one-line note tucked under a pillow that had grown cold: *I'm sorry, but this just isn't going to work.*

That was it. No explanation, no real indication of remorse. The note had been as clinical and compassionless as an eviction notice, which, in effect, it had been, Natalie thought as she navigated through the morning traffic. Matt had written the note to evict her from his life.

She'd spent the next two weeks crying, breaking down without warning as she walked down the street, or as she sat staring at a meal she couldn't bring herself to eat.

Candace, she remembered with a bittersweet pang, had tried to get her to go clubbing in order to get her to forget about Matt.

She'd turned her twin down, but she did get her act together. If Matt didn't think enough of their relationship to try to contact her, to try to make her understand why he'd changed so radically from lover to stranger,

then to hell with him. He was dead to her, she resolved.
And he'd remained that way.

Until twenty minutes ago.

The adrenaline in her veins kept mounting.

Natalie focused on her driving. Vegas in the daylight
wasn't nearly as alluring, as magical and glitzy as it was
after dark. Like an aging woman best seen in soft lighting,
Vegas's imperfections were all visible in the daylight.
Natalie supposed that was why people like her sister
didn't like to get up until noon. They lived for the night.

Except that Candace could no longer do that.

The thought brought a fresh, sharp ache with it.

"Dammit, Candy, what a waste," Natalie murmured
under her breath.

She pulled up before the Janus casino. One of the
three valets currently on duty came to life and made a
beeline for her vehicle.

"Welcome to the Janus," the young attendant said
cheerfully as he opened her door with a flourish.

"We'll see," she replied solemnly.

As he pulled away with her car, Natalie looked up at
the casino's logo. Janus was the Roman god with two
faces, one pointed toward the past, the other facing the
future. It struck her as rather ironic, given what she was
doing here, seeking out someone from her past in order
to get answers so that the future could be settled.

The moment she entered the casino, the Vegas phe-
nomena took hold. It was like stepping into a world
where time did not matter or even make an appearance.
There was only a sense of "now."

Because in Natalie's experience she'd discovered

that bartenders knew the inner workings of any establishment they worked for better than anyone else, she made her way to the first bar she saw within the casino.

The bartender in attendance was a gregarious man in his early forties. He had a quick, sexy smile, which was probably one of the main reasons he'd been hired. His name tag identified him as Kevin.

Moving to her end of the bar, Kevin asked, "What'll it be, pretty lady?"

"Information." She saw a dubious look cross his brow. To counter that, she took out her badge. Granted she wasn't here in an official capacity, but Kevin didn't need to know that. "Were you on duty last night?"

Kevin began to wipe the gleaming black surface of the bar. "You mean, during the gala?"

"Yes."

The smile gracing his lips was a satisfied one. Last night had obviously been profitable for him, she judged. "I caught an extra shift."

She took out Candace's photograph and carefully placed it on the bar. "Did you happen to see this woman there?"

The bartender glanced at the picture. Mild interest turned to recognition. "You mean, Candace Rothchild? Yeah, she was here, loud and brassy as always. But not for long," he added, looking rather disappointed. There was always a circus when Candace was around, Natalie thought. "She and the boss had at it and then he had our head of security escort her out."

She latched on to the first part of his statement. "They argued? About what?"

He shook his head. "Couldn't tell you. Too far away for anything but body language," he confessed.

"And the head of security?" she asked.

"He got her to leave."

She leaned in over the bar. "Tell me about him."

"Don't know much," the bartender admitted. "Just that his name's Matt Shaffer. Boss flew him in from L.A. where he was head of security for Montgomery Enterprises."

There was no avoiding it, she thought darkly. She was going to have to talk to Matt. The thought left her cold. "Do you know where I can find him right now?"

Kevin glanced at his watch. "He should be in his office. On the second floor, toward the rear." He gave her the numbers of the rooms where the monitors that kept watch over the casino guests as they tried their luck against the house were located.

Taking out a twenty, she placed it on the bar. "Thanks for your help."

Kevin slipped the bill into his vest pocket. "Anytime, lovely lady," he called after her. "Anytime."

She debated going up the stairs, then decided on the elevator. The car that took her up to the second floor was empty. Natalie stepped out of the elevator, looked around to get her bearings and then walked toward the rear of the floor.

"Into the Valley of Death rode the six hundred," she silently recited, digging deep for a line from a poem by Tennyson. Wrapping her hand around a brass handle, she opened one of the glass doors and walked in.

The woman whose desk was closest to the door

looked up. "You can't come in here. This is a re-
stricted area."

Natalie already had her ID in her hand and held it up.
"I'm looking for Matt Shaffer," she told the woman.

God, even saying his name made her mouth go dry.
She was supposed to be over him, to have moved on
with her life. What happened?

The woman began to answer her. "He's—"

"Right here."

The deep voice came from behind her. Natalie felt
every single nerve ending go on tactical alert at the
same moment that all the hairs at the back of her neck
stood up. Eight years had passed, but she would have
recognized his voice anywhere.

* * * * *

CELEBRATE
60 YEARS
OF PURE READING PLEASURE
WITH HARLEQUIN®!

Look for Silhouette®
Romantic Suspense in April!

Love In 60 Seconds

Bright lights. Big city. Hearts in overdrive.

Silhouette® Romantic Suspense is celebrating
Harlequin's 60th Anniversary with six stories that
promise to bring readers the glitz of Las Vegas,
the danger of revenge, the mystery of a missing
diamond, and family scandals.

www.eHarlequin.com   SRS60BPA

You're invited to join our Tell Harlequin Reader Panel!

By joining our new reader panel you will:

- Receive Harlequin® books—they are FREE and yours to keep with no obligation to purchase anything!
- Participate in fun online surveys
- Exchange opinions and ideas with women just like you
- Have a say in our new book ideas and help us publish the best in women's fiction

*In addition, you will have a chance to win great prizes and receive special gifts!
See Web site for details. Some conditions apply.
Space is limited.*

To join, visit us at

www.TellHarlequin.com.

NEW YORK TIMES
BESTSELLING AUTHOR

CARLA NEGGERS

A red velvet bag holding
ten sparkling gems.

A woman who must
confront their legacy
of deceit, scandal and murder.

Rebecca Blackburn caught a glimpse of the famed
Jupiter Stones as a small child. Unaware of their
significance, she forgot about them—until a
seemingly innocent photograph reignites one man's
simmering desire for vengeance.

Rebecca turns to Jared Sloan, the love she lost to
tragedy and scandal, his own life changed forever
by the secrets buried deep in their two families.
Their relentless quest for the truth will dredge up
bitter memories...and they will stop at nothing to
expose a cold-blooded killer.

BETRAYALS

*Available February 24, 2009,
wherever books are sold!*

MIRA®

Silhouette®
Romantic
SUSPENSE

COMING NEXT MONTH

Available March 31, 2009

#1555 PROTECTOR OF ONE—Rachel Lee
Conard County: The Next Generation
When Kerry Tomlinson has visions of a local murder, she turns to the police and retired DCI agent Adrian Goddard. He doesn't want to get involved, but his sense of duty compels him to protect her when someone finds out she's helping the police. As the killers draw closer, Kerry and Adrian must confront their own issues if they want to save each other.

#1556 THE HEIRESS'S 2-WEEK AFFAIR—Marie Ferrarella
Love in 60 Seconds
Her twin sister murdered, a priceless diamond ring missing and her former lover, Matt Shaffer, back in town—Las Vegas detective Natalie Rothchild's world has come unraveled. And now she must work with Matt in the face of danger to find her sister's killer and discover whether her heart can open to him again.

#1557 THE PERFECT SOLDIER—Karen Whiddon
The Cordasic Legacy
Military spy Sebastian Cordasic returned from war a changed man. Assigned to protect country music superstar Jillian Everhart from terrorists, he never expected to feel emotions for her. But when Jillian is taken by the same men who tortured him, Sebastian must face his past to rescue the woman he now can't live without.

#1558 IN SAFE HANDS—Linda Conrad
The Safekeepers
On a mission to find relatives of the orphaned baby she wants to adopt, Maggie Ryan locates the uncle, Colin Fairfax. But the drug lord who killed the child's parents finds Colin, too—and he wants him dead. Maggie and Colin join forces for protection, but they fail to protect their hearts against their growing attraction.

SRSCNMBPA0309